The Red Seal

Natalie Sumner Lincoln

Contents

THE RED SEAL

BY

Natalie Sumner Lincoln

THE RED SEAL
by Natalie Sumner Lincoln

CHAPTER I. IN THE POLICE COURT

Te Assistant District Attorney glanced down at the papers in his hand and then up at the well-dressed, stockily built man occupying the witness stand. His manner was conciliatory.

"According to your testimony, Mr. Clymer, the prisoner, John Sylvester, was honest and reliable, and faithfully performed his duties as confidential clerk," he stated. "Just when was Sylvester in your employ?"

"Sylvester was never in my employ," corrected Benjamin Augustus Clymer. The president of the Metropolis Trust Company was noted for his precision of speech. "During the winter of 1918 I shared an apartment with Judge James Hildebrand, who employed Sylvester."

"Was Sylvester addicted to drink?"

"No."

"Was he quarrelsome?"

"No."

"Was Sylvester married at that date?"

At the question a faint smile touched the corners of Clymer's clean shaven mouth and his eyes traveled involuntarily toward the over-dressed female whose charge of assault and battery against her husband had brought Clymer to the police court as a "character" witness in Sylvester's behalf.

"Sylvester left Judge Hildebrand to get married," he explained. "He was a model clerk; honest, sober, and industrious."

"That is all, Mr. Clymer." The Assistant District Attorney spoke in some haste. "You may retire, sir," and, as Clymer turned to vacate the witness box, he addressed the presiding judge.

Clymer did not catch his remarks as, on stepping down, he was button-holed by a man whose entrance had occurred a few minutes before through the swing door which gave exit from the space reserved for witnesses and lawyers into the body of the court room.

"Sit over here a second," the newcomer said in an undertone, indicating the long bench under the window. "Has Miss McIntyre been here?"

"Miss McIntyre--here?" Clymer stared in amazement at his questioner. "No, certainly not."

"Don't be so positive," retorted the lawyer heatedly, his color rising at the other's incredulous tone. "Helen McIntyre telephoned me to meet her, and--by Jove, here she comes," as a slight stir at the back of the court room caused him to glance in that direction.

A gray-haired patrolman, cap in hand, was in the lead of the small procession which filed up the aisle, and Clymer gazed in astonishment at Helen McIntyre and her twin sister, Barbara. What had brought them at that hour to the police court?

The court room was filled with men, both white and black, while a dozen or more slatternly negro women were seated here and there. The Assistant District Attorney's plea for a postponement of the Sylvester case on the ground of the absence of an important witness and the granting of his plea was entirely lost on the majority of those in the court room, their attention being wholly centered on Helen McIntyre and Barbara, whose bearing and clothes spoke of a fashionable and prosperous world to which nearly all present were utterly foreign.

Barbara, sensitive to the concentrated regard which their entrance had attracted, drew closer to Dr. Amos Stone, their family physician, who had accompanied them at her particular request. Except for Mrs. Sylvester, she and her sister were the only white women in the room.

Before they could take the seats to which they had been ushered, the clerk's stentorian tones sent the girls' names echoing down the court room and Barbara, much perturbed, found herself standing with Helen before the clerk's desk. There was a moment's wait and the deputy marshal, who had motioned to one of the prisoners sitting in the "cage" to step outside, emphasized his order with a muttered imprecation to hurry. A slouching figure finally shambled past him and stopped some little distance from the group in front of the Judge's bench.

"House-breaking," announced the clerk. "Charge brought by--" He looked up at the two girls.

"Miss Helen McIntyre," answered one of the twins composedly. "Daughter of Colonel Charles McIntyre of this city."

"Charge brought by Miss Helen McIntyre," continued the clerk, "against--" and his pointed finger indicated the seedy looking man slouching before them.

"Smith," said the latter, and his husky voice was barely audible.

"Smith," repeated the clerk. "First name--?"

"John," was the answer, given after a slight pause.

"John Smith, you are charged by Miss Helen McIntyre with house-breaking. What say you--guilty or not guilty?"

The man shifted his weight from one foot to the other and shot an uneasy look about him.

"Not guilty," he responded.

At that instant Helen caught sight of Benjamin Clymer and his companion, Philip Rochester, and her pale cheeks flushed faintly at the lawyer's approach. He had time but for a hasty handshake before the clerk administered the oath to the prisoner and the witnesses in the case.

Rochester walked back and resumed his seat by Clymer. Propping himself in the corner made by the bench and the cage, inside of which sat the prisoners, he opened his right hand and unfolded a small paper. He read the brief penciled message it contained not once but a dozen times. Folding the paper into minute dimensions he tucked it carefully inside his vest pocket and glanced sideways at Clymer. The banker hardly noticed his uneasy movements as he sat regarding Helen McIntyre standing in the witness box. Although paler than usual, the girl's manner was quiet, but Clymer, a close student of human nature, decided she was keeping her composure by will power alone, and his interest grew.

The Judge, from the Bench, was also regarding the handsome witness and the burglar with close attention. Colonel Charles McIntyre, a wealthy manufacturer, had, upon his retirement from active business, made the National Capital his home, and his name had become a household word for philanthropy, while his twin daughters were both popular in Washington's gay younger set. Several reporters of local papers, attracted by the mention of the McIntyre name, as well as by the twins' appearance, watched the scene with keen expectancy, eager for early morning "copy."

As the Assistant District Attorney rose to question Helen McIntyre, the Judge addressed him.

"Is the prisoner represented by counsel?" he asked.

For reply the burglar shook his head. Rising slowly to his feet, Philip Rochester advanced to the man's side.

"If it please the court," he began, "I will take the case for the prisoner."

His offer received a quick acceptance from the Bench, but the scowl with which the burglar favored him was not pleasant. Hitching at his frayed flannel collar, the man partly turned his back on the lawyer and listened with a heavy frown to Helen's quick answers to the questions put to her.

"While waiting for my sister to return from a dance early this morning," she stated, "I went downstairs into the library, and as I entered it I saw a man slip across the room and into a coat closet. I retained enough presence of mind to steal across to the closet and turn the key in the door; then I ran to the window and fortunately saw Officer O'Ryan standing under the arc light across the street. I called him and he arrested the prisoner."

Her simple statement evoked a nod of approval from the Assistant District Attorney, and Rochester frowned as he waived his right to cross-examine her. The next witness was Officer O'Ryan, and his testimony confirmed Helen's.

"The prisoner was standing back among the coats in the closet," he said. "My automatic against his ribs brought him out."

"Did you search your prisoner?" asked Rochester, as he took the witness.

"Yes, sir.

"Find any concealed weapons?"

"No, sir."

"A burglar's kit?"

"No, sir."

"Did the prisoner make a statement after his arrest?"

"No, sir; he came along peaceably enough, hardly a word out of him," acknowledged O'Ryan regretfully. He enjoyed a reputation on the force as a "scrapper," and a willing prisoner was a disappointment to his naturally pugnacious disposition.

"Did you search the house?"

"Sure, and haven't I been telling you I did?" answered O'Ryan; his pride in his achievement in arresting a burglar in so fashionable a neighborhood as Sheridan Circle was giving place to resentment at Rochester's manner of addressing him. At a sign from the lawyer, he left the witness stand, and Rochester addressed the Judge.

"I ask the indulgence of the court for more time," he commenced, "that I may consult my client and find if he desires to call witnesses."

"The court finds," responded the Judge, "that a clear case of house-breaking has been proven against the prisoner by reputable witnesses. He will have to stand trial."

For the first time the prisoner raised his eyes from contemplation of the floor.

"I demand trial by jury," he announced.

"It is your right," acknowledged the Judge, and turned to consult his calendar.

Stepping forward, the deputy marshal laid his hand on the burglar's shoulder.

"Go inside," he directed and held open the cage door, which immediately swung back into place, and Rochester, following closely at the prisoner's heels, halted abruptly. A fit of coughing shook the burglar and he paused by the iron railing, gasping for breath.

"Water," he pleaded, and a court attendant handed a cup to Rochester, standing just outside the cage, and he passed it over the iron railing to the burglar. Then turning on his heel the lawyer rejoined Clymer, his discontent plainly discernible.

"A clear case against your client," remarked Clymer, reading his thoughts. "Don't take the affair to heart, man; you did your best under difficulties."

Rochester shook his head gloomily. "I might have--Jove! why didn't I ask for bail?"

"Bail!" The banker suppressed a chuckle as he eyed the threadbare suit and tattered appearance of the burglar, who had resumed his seat in the prisoner's cage. "Who would have stood surety for that scarecrow?"

"I would have." Rochester spoke with some vehemence, but his words were partly drowned by the violent fit of coughing which again shook the burglar, and before he could finish his sentence, Helen McIntyre stood at his elbow. She bowed gravely to Clymer who rose at her approach, and laid a persuasive hand on Rochester's sleeve.

"Will you come with us?" she asked. "Barbara and Dr. Stone are ready to leave. The doctor wishes to--" As she spoke she looked across at Stone, who stood opposite her in the little group. He failed to catch both her word and her eye, his gaze, passing over her shoulder, was riveted on the burglar.

"Something is wrong," he announced and pushed past Barbara. "Let me inside the cage," he directed as the deputy marshal kept the gate closed at his approach. "Your prisoner appears ill."

One glance at the burglar proved the truth of the physician's statement and the gate was hastily opened. Stone bent over the man, whose spasmodic breathing could be heard distinctly through the court room, then his gaze shifted to the other occupants of the cage.

"The man must have air," he declared. "Your aid here." Looking up his eyes met Clymer's, and the latter came swiftly into the cage, followed by Rochester, and the deputy marshal slammed the door shut behind them.

"Step out this way," he said, as Clymer aided the physician in lifting the burglar, and he led them into the ante-room whence prisoners were taken into the cage.

Stretching his burden on the floor, Stone tore open the man's shirt and felt his heart, while Clymer, spying a water cooler, sped across the room and returned immediately with a brimming glass.

"Here's water," he said, but Stone refused the proffered glass.

"No use," he announced. "The man is dead."

"Dead!" echoed the deputy marshal. "Well, I'll be--say, doctor," but Stone had darted out of the room, and he turned open-mouthed to Clymer. "If it wasn't Doctor Stone I would say he was crazy," he declared.

"Tut! Feel the man's heart and convince yourself," suggested Clymer tartly, and the deputy marshal, dropping on one knee, did so. Detecting no heart-beat, the officer passed his hand over the dead man's unshaven chin and across his forehead, brushing back the unkempt hair. Under his none too gentle touch the wig slipped back, revealing to his astonished gaze a head of short cropped, red hair.

Clymer, who had followed the deputy marshal's movements with interest, gave a shout which was echoed by Rochester and Dr. Stone, who returned at that moment.

"Good God!" gasped Clymer, shaken out of his accustomed calm. "Jimmie Turnbull!"

The deputy marshal eyed the startled men.

"You don't mean--" he stammered, and paused.

For answer Dr. Stone straightened the dead man and removed the wig.

"James Turnbull," he said gravely, and turning, addressed Rochester, who had dropped down on the nearest chair. "Cashier of the Metropolis Trust Company, Rochester, and your roommate, masquerading as a burglar."

CHAPTER II. THE GAME OF CONSEQUENCES

R. O. Chester did not appear to hear Dr. Stone's words. With eyes half starting from their sockets he sat staring at the dead man, completely oblivious of the others' presence. After watching him for a moment the physician turned briskly to the dazed deputy marshal.

"Summon the coroner," he directed. "We cannot move the body until he comes."

His curt tone brought the official's wits back with a jump and he made for the exit, only to be stopped at the threshold by a sandy-haired man just entering the room.

At the word coroner, Rochester raised himself from his bent attitude and brushed his hand across his eyes.

"No need for a coroner to diagnose the case," he objected. "Poor Turnbull always said he would go off like that."

Stone moved nearer. "Like that?" he questioned, pointing to the still figure. "Explain yourself, Rochester. Did Turnbull expect to die here in this manner?"

"No--no--certainly not." The lawyer moistened his dry lips. "But when a man has angina pectoris he knows the end may come at any moment and in any place. Turnbull made no secret of suffering from that disease." Rochester turned toward Clymer. "You knew it."

Benjamin Clymer, who had been gazing alternately at the dead man and vague-ly about the room, looked startled at the abrupt question.

"I knew Turnbull had bad attacks of the heart; we all knew it at the bank," he stated. "But I understood the disease had responded to treatment."

"There is no cure for angina pectoris," declared Rochester.

"No permanent cure," amended Stone, and would have added more, but Roch-ester stopped him.

"Now that you know Turnbull died of angina pectoris there is no necessity of sending for the coroner," Rochester spoke in haste, his words tumbling over each other. "I will go at once and communicate with an undertaker." But before he could rise from his chair the sandy-haired man, who had conducted a whispered conver-sation with the deputy marshal, advanced toward the group.

"Just a moment, gentlemen," he said, and turned back a lapel of his coat and displayed a metal badge. "I am Ferguson of the Central Office. Do you know the deceased?"

"He was my intimate friend," announced Rochester before his companions could reply to the detective's question, which was addressed to all. "Mr. Clymer, here, can tell you that Jimmie Turnbull, cashier of his bank, was well known in financial and social Washington."

"How came he here in this fix?" asked Ferguson with more force than gram-matic clarity.

"A sudden heart attack--angina pectoris, you know," replied Rochester glibly, "with fatal results."

"I wasn't alluding to what killed him," Ferguson explained. "But why was the cashier of the Metropolis Trust Company," he looked questioningly at Clymer whom he knew quite well by sight, "and a social high-light, decked out in these clothes and a wig, too?" leaning down, the better to examine the clothing on the dead man.

"He had just been held for the Grand Jury on a charge of house-breaking," vol-unteered the deputy marshal. "I reckon that brought on his heart-attack."

"True, true," agreed Rochester. "The excitement was too much for him."

"House-breaking" ejaculated the detective. "Dangerous sport for a man suffer-ing with angina pectoris, aside from anything else. Who preferred charges?"

"The Misses McIntyre," answered the deputy marshal, to whom the question was addressed. "Like to interview them?"

"Yes."

"No, no!" Rochester was on his feet instantly. "There is no necessity to bring the twins out here--it's too tragic!"

"Tragic?" echoed Ferguson. "Why?"

"Why--why--Turnbull was arrested in their house," Rochester was commencing to stutter. "He was their friend--"

"Caught burglarizing, heh?" Ferguson's eyes glowed; the case already whetted his remarkably keen inquisitorial instinct which had gained him place and certain fame in the Washington police force. "Are the Misses McIntyre still in the building?"

"They were in the court room just before we brought Turnbull's body here," responded the deputy marshal. "I guess they are still waiting, eh, doctor?"

Stone, thus appealed to, nodded. "I agree with Mr. Rochester," he said, and the gravity of his manner impressed Ferguson. "It is better for me to break the news of Mr. Turnbull's death to the young ladies before bringing them here. Therefore, with your permission, Ferguson"--He got no further.

Through the outer entrance of the room came Helen McIntyre and her sister Barbara, conducted by the same bowing patrolman who had ushered them into the court room an hour before.

"My God! Too late!" stammered Rochester under his breath, and he turned in desperation to Benjamin Clymer. The bank president's state of mind at the extraordinary masquerade and sudden death of his popular and trusted cashier bordered on shocked horror, which had made him a passive witness of the rapidly shifting scene. Rochester clutched his arm in his agitation. "Get the twins out of here--do something, man! Don't you know that Turnbull was in love with--"

His fervid whisper penetrated further than he realized and one of the McIntyre twins looked inquiringly in their direction. Clymer, more startled than his demeanor indicated, wondered if she had overheard Rochester's ejaculations, but whatever action the banker contemplated in response to the lawyer's appeal was checked by a scream from the girl on his right. With ashen face and trembling finger she pointed to Turnbull's body which suddenly confronted her as she walked forward.

"Who is it?" she gasped. "Babs, tell me!" And she held out her hand imploringly.

Her sister stepped to her side and bent over Turnbull. When she looked up her lips alone retained their color.

"Hush!" she implored, giving her sister a slight shake. "Hush! It is Jimmie Turnbull. Can you not see for yourself, dear?"

It seemed doubtful if Helen heard her; with attention wholly centered on the dead man she swayed on her feet, and Dr. Stone, thinking she was about to fall, placed a supporting arm about her.

"Do you not know Jimmie?" asked her sister. "Don't stare so, dearest." Her tone was pleading.

"Perhaps the young lady has some difficulty in recognizing Mr. Turnbull in his disguise," suggested Ferguson, who stood somewhat in the background but closely observing the scene.

"Disguise!" Helen raised her eyes and Ferguson, hardened as he had become to tragic scenes, felt a throb of pity as he caught the pent-up agony in her mute appeal.

"Yes, Miss," he said awkwardly. "The burglar you caught in your house was Mr. Turnbull in disguise."

Barbara McIntyre released her grasp of her sister's arm and collapsed on a chair. Stone, still supporting Helen, felt her muscles grow taut and an instant later she stepped back from his side and stood by her sister. As the two girls faced the circle of men, the likeness between them was extraordinary. Each had the same slight graceful figure, equal height; and feature for feature, coloring matching coloring, they were identical; their gowns, even, were cut on similar lines, only their hats varied in shape and color.

"Do I understand, gentlemen," Helen began, and her voice gained steadiness as she proceeded, "that the burglar whom Officer O'Ryan and I caught lurking in our house was James Turnbull?"

"He was," answered Ferguson, and Stone, as the twins looked dumbly at him, confirmed the detective's statement with a brief, "Yes."

The silence that ensued was broken by Barbara rising to her feet.

"Jimmie won his wager," she announced. Her gaze did not waver before the concentrated regard of the men facing her. "He broke into our house--but, oh, how can I pay my debt to him now that he is dead!"

"Hush!" Helen laid a cautioning hand on her sister's arm as the latter's voice gained in shrillness, the shrillness of approaching hysteria.

"I am all right, Helen." Barbara waved her away impatiently. "What caused Jimmie's death?"

"Angina pectoris," declared Rochester. "Too much excitement brought on a fatal attack." Barbara nodded dazedly. "I knew he had heart trouble, but--" She stepped toward Turnbull and her voice quivered with feeling. "Don't leave Jimmie lying there; take him to his room, doctor," turning entreatingly to Stone.

The physician looked at her compassionately. "I will, just as soon as the coroner views the body," he promised. "But come away now, Babs; this is no place for you and Helen." He signed to the deputy marshal to open the door as he walked across the room, Barbara keeping step with him, and her sister following in their wake. At the door Barbara paused and looked back.

"Will there be an inquest?" she asked.

"That's for the coroner to decide," responded Ferguson. "As long as Mr. Turnbull entered your house on a wager and died from an attack of angina pectoris the inquest is likely to be a mere formality. Ah, here is the coroner now," as a man paused in the doorway.

Helen McIntyre moved back from the door to make room for Coroner Penfield. Having had occasion to attend court that morning, he was passing the door when attracted by the group just inside the room. Courteously acknowledging Helen's act, Penfield stepped briskly across the threshold and stopped abruptly on catching sight of the lonely figure on the floor.

"Won't you hold an autopsy, Ferguson?" asked Clymer, breaking his long silence.

"No, sir, we never do when the cause of death is apparent," the detective bowed to Coroner Penfield. "Isn't that so, Coroner?"

Penfield nodded. "Unless the condition of the body indicates foul play or the relatives specially request it, we do not perform autopsies," he answered. "What has happened here?" and he gazed about with quickened interest.

"Mr. Turnbull, who masqueraded as a burglar on a wager with Miss McIntyre died suddenly from angina pectoris," explained the deputy marshal.

"Just a case of death from natural causes," broke in Rochester. "Please write out a permit for me to remove Turnbull's body, Dr. Penfield."

Helen McIntyre took a step forward. Her eyes, twice their accustomed size, shone brightly, in contrast to her dead white face. Carefully avoiding her sister's glance she addressed the coroner.

"I must insist," she began and stopped to control her voice. "As Mr. Turnbull's fiancee, I--" she faltered again. "I demand that an autopsy be held to determine the cause of his death."

CHAPTER III. THE ROOM WITH THE SEVEN DOORS

Mrs. Brewster regarded her surroundings with inward satisfaction. It would have taken a far more captious critic than the pretty widow to find fault with the large, high-ceilinged room in which she sat. The handsome carved Venetian furniture, the rich hangings and valuable paintings on the walls gave evidence of Colonel McIntyre's artistic taste and appreciation of the beautiful. Mrs. Brewster had never failed, during her visit to the McIntyre twins, to examine the rare curios in the carved cabinets and the tapestries on the walls, but that afternoon, with one eye on the clock and the other on her embroidery, she sat waiting in growing impatience for the interruption she anticipated.

The hands of the clock had passed the hour of five before the buzz of a distant bell brought her to her feet. Hurrying to the window she peeped between the curtains in time to see a stylish roadster electric glide down the driveway leading from the McIntyre residence and stop at the curb. As she turned to go back to her chair Dr. Stone was ushered into the library by the footman. Mrs. Brewster welcomed her cousin with frank relief.

"I have waited so impatiently for you," she confessed, making room for him to sit on the sofa by her side.

"I was detained, Margaret." Stone's voice was not over-cordial; three imperative telephone calls from her, coming at a moment when he had been engaged with a serious case in his office, had provoked him. "Do you wish to see me professionally?"

"Indeed, I don't." She laughed frankly. "I am the picture of health."

Stone, observing her fine coloring and clear eyes, silently agreed with her. The widow made a charming picture in her modish tea-gown, and the physician, watching her with an appraising eye, acknowledged the beauty which had captivated all Washington. Mrs. Brewster had carried her honors tactfully, a fact which had gained her popularity even among the dowagers and match-making mothers who take an active part in Washington's social season.

"Then, Margaret, what do you wish to see me about?" Stone asked, after waiting without result for her to continue speaking.

She laughed softly. "You are the most practical of men," she said. "It would not have been so difficult to find a companion anxious to spend the whole afternoon with me for my sake alone."

"Colonel McIntyre, for instance?" he teased, and laughed amusedly at her heightened color. "Have a care, Margaret; McIntyre's flirtations are all very well, but he is the type of man to be deadly in earnest when once he falls in love."

"Thanks for your warning," Mrs. Brewster smiled, then grew serious. "I sent for you to ask about Jimmie Turnbull's death this morning. Barbara told me you accompanied them to the police court."

"Yes. Why weren't you with the girls?"

"Because I was told nothing of their trip to the police court until they had returned," she replied. "How horribly tragic the whole affair is!" And a shiver she could not suppress crept down her spine.

"It is," agreed Stone. "What possessed Jimmie Turnbull to play so mad a trick?"

"His wager with Barbara."

Stone leaned a little nearer. "Have you learned the nature of that wager?" he asked, lowering his voice.

"No. Babs was in so hysterical a condition when she returned from the police court that she gave a very incoherent account of the whole affair, and she has kept her room ever since luncheon," explained Mrs. Brewster.

Stone looked puzzled. "I understood that Jimmie was attentive to Helen McIntyre and not to Barbara," he said. "But upon my word, Barbara appeared more over-come by Jimmie's death than Helen."

Mrs. Brewster did not reply at once; instead, she glanced carefully around. The room was generally the rallying place of the McIntyres. It stretched across almost the entire width of the house; the diamond-paned and recessed windows gave it a medieval air in keeping with its antique furniture, and the seven doors opening from it led, respectively, to the large dining room beyond, a morning room, billiard room, the front and back halls, and the Italian loggia which over-looked the stretch of ground between the McIntyre residence and its neighbor on the north. Apparently, she and Dr. Stone had the room to themselves.

"I cannot answer your question with positiveness," she stated. "Frankly, Jim-mie appeared impartial in his attentions to the twins. When he wasn't with Barbara he was with Helen, and vice versa."

Stone gazed at her in some perplexity. "Are you aware that Helen stated at the police court this morning that she was Turnbull's fiancee?"

"What!" Mrs. Brewster actually bounced in her seat. "You--you astound me!"

"I was a bit surprised myself," acknowledged the physician. "I thought Roch-ester--however, that is neither here nor there. Helen not only announced she was Jimmie's fiancee but as such demanded that a post-mortem examination be held to determine the cause of his death."

Mrs. Brewster's pretty color faded and the glance she turned on her cousin was sharp. "Why should Helen suspect foul play?" she demanded. "For that is what her request hinted."

"True." Stone pulled his beard absentmindedly. "Ah, here is Colonel McIn-tyre," he exclaimed as the portieres before the hall door parted and a tall man strode into the library.

McIntyre was a favorite with the old physician, and he welcomed his arrival with warmth. Exchanging a word of greeting with Mrs. Brewster, McIntyre drew up a chair and dropped into it.

"I called at your office, doctor," he said. "Went there at once on learning the shocking news about poor Turnbull. Why in the world didn't he announce who he was when my daughter had him arrested as a burglar? He must have realized that prolonged excitement was bad for his weak heart."

Mrs. Brewster, who had settled herself more comfortably in her corner of the sofa on McIntyre's arrival, answered his remark.

"I only knew Jimmie superficially," she said, "but he had one distinguishing trait patent to all, his inordinate fondness for practical jokes. Probably the predicament he found himself in was highly to his taste--until his heart failed."

Her voice, slightly raised, carried across the room and reached the ears of a tall, slender girl who had stood hesitating on the threshold of the dining worn door on beholding the group by the sofa. All hesitation vanished, however, as the meaning of Mrs. Brewster's remark dawned on her, and she walked over to the sofa.

"You are very unjust, Margaret," she stated, and at sound of her low triante voice McIntyre whirled around and frowned slightly. "Jimmie was thinking of the predicament of others, not of himself."

"What do you mean, Helen?" her father demanded.

"Why, how could Jimmie reveal his identity in court without involving us?" she asked. "Good afternoon, doctor," recollecting her manners, and her attention thus diverted, she missed the sudden questioning look which Mrs. Brewster and her father exchanged. "No," she continued, "Jimmie sacrificed himself for others."

"By becoming a burglar." McIntyre laughed shortly. "Don't talk arrant nonsense, Helen."

The girl flushed at his tone, and Dr. Stone, an interested onlooker, marveled at the fleeting flash of disdain which lighted her dark eyes. Stone's interest grew. The McIntyre family had always been particularly congenial, and the devotion of Colonel McIntyre (left a widower when the twins were in short frocks) to his daughters had been commented on frequently by their wide circle of friends in Washington and by acquaintances made in their travels abroad.

Colonel McIntyre had married when quite a young man. Frugality and industry and a brilliant mind had reaped their reward, and, wiser than the majority of Americans, he retired early from business and devoted himself to a life of leisure and the education of his daughters. Their debut the previous autumn had been one of the social events of the Washington season, and the instant popularity the girls had attained proved a source of pride to Colonel McIntyre. His chief pleasure consisted in gratifying their every whim, and Dr. Stone, knowing the family as he did, wondered at the faintly discernible air of constraint in the girl's manner. Usually frank to a sometimes embarrassing degree, she appeared to some disadvantage as she sat gazing moodily at the tips of her patent-leather pumps. Dr. Stone's attention shifted to Colonel McIntyre and lastly to the pretty widow at his elbow. Had Dame Rumor spoken truly in the report, widely circulated, that the colonel had fallen a victim to the charms of Margaret Brewster, his daughters' guest? If so, it might account for the young girl's manner--however devoted McIntyre's daughters might be to Mrs. Brewster as a friend and companion, they might resent having so young a woman for their step-mother.

Not receiving any reply to his remarks, McIntyre was about to address his daughter again when she spoke.

"Jimmie will be justified," she declared stoutly. "Has the coroner held the autopsy yet, Dr. Stone?"

"Autopsy!" McIntyre spoke with sharp abruptness. "I thought it was clearly established that Jimmie died from angina pectoris?"

"It is so believed," responded Stone. His mystification was growing; had not Helen informed her father of the scene which had transpired at the police court, and of her request to the coroner? "I understand the post-mortem examination will be made this afternoon, Helen."

A heavy paper knife, nicely balanced between McIntyre's well manicured fingers, dropped to the floor as a step sounded behind him and the butler, Grimes, stopped by his side.

"Mr. Rochester just telephoned that his partner, Mr. Harry Kent, is out of town, Miss"--bowing to the silent girl. Grimes always contented himself with addressing his "young ladies" by the simple prefix "Miss," and never added their given names, because, as he expressed it, "them twins are alike as two peas, and which is which, I dunno." Considering himself one of the family from his long service with Colonel McIntyre, he kept a watchful eye on the twins, but their pranks in childhood had often exasperated him into giving notice, which he generally found it convenient to forget when the first of a new month came around.

"Mr. Kent will be back to-morrow," added the butler, as silence followed the delivery of his message. "Mr. Rochester wishes to know if he can transact any business for you."

"Please thank him and say no." The girl's color rose as she caught her father's disapproving look. The colonel waited until the butler had disappeared before addressing her.

"Why did you send for Harry Kent?" he questioned. "You know I do not approve of his attentions to Barbara. Rochester is well enough--"

"Speaking of Rochester"--Mrs. Brewster saw the gathering storm clouds in the girl's expressive eyes, and broke hastily into the conversation. "I see by the paper, Cousin Amos"--she turned so as to face Dr. Stone-- "that Mr. Rochester declared positively that Jimmie Turnbull died from angina pectoris."

"What's Philip's opinion worth?" The young girl smiled disdainfully. "Philip seems to think that having shared an apartment with Jimmie, gives him intimate knowledge of Jimmie's health. Philip is not a medical man."

"No," acknowledged her father. "But here is a medical man who was on the spot when Jimmie died. What's your opinion, Stone?"

Stone, suddenly conscious of the keen attention of his companions, spoke slowly as was his wont when making a serious statement.

"Rochester's contention that Jimmie died from angina pectoris would seem borne out by what transpired," he said. "Undoubtedly Jimmie felt an attack coming on and used the customary remedy to relieve it--"

"And what was that remedy?" questioned Mrs. Brewster swiftly.

"Amyl nitrite." Stone spoke with decision. "I could detect its presence by the fruity, pleasant odor which always accompanies the drug's use."

"Ah!" The exclamation slipped from Mrs. Brewster. "Is the drug administered in water?"

"No, it is inhaled--take care, you have dropped your handkerchief." Stone pulled himself up short in his speech, and bent over but the young girl was too quick for him, and stooped first to pick up her handkerchief.

As she raised her head Stone caught sight of the tiny mole under the lobe of her left ear. It was the one mark which distinguished Barbara from her twin sister. Colonel McIntyre had addressed his daughter as Helen, and she had not undeceived him--Why? The perplexed physician gave up the problem.

"The drug," he went on to explain, "amyl nitrite comes in pearl capsules and is crushed in a handkerchief and the fumes inhaled."

Mrs. Brewster leaned forward suddenly. "Would that cause death?" she asked.

Stone shook his head in denial. "Not the customary dose of three minims," he answered, and turning, found that Barbara had stolen from the room.

CHAPTER IV. BARBARA ENGAGES COUNSEL

Bidding a hasty good morning to the elevator girl, Harry Kent, suit-case in hand, entered the cage and was carried up to the fourth floor of the Wilkins Building. Several business acquaintances stopped to chat with him as he walked down the corridor to his office, and it was fully fifteen minutes before he turned the knob of the door bearing the firm name--ROCHESTER AND KENT, ATTORNEYS--on its glass panel. As he stepped inside the anteroom which separated the two offices occupied respectively by him and his senior partner, Philip Rochester, a stranger rose from the clerk's desk.

"Yes, sir?" he asked interrogatively.

Kent eyed him in surprise. "Mr. Rochester here?" he inquired.

"No, sir. It am in charge of the office."

"You are!" Kent's surprise increased. "I happen to be Mr. Kent, junior partner in this firm."

"I beg your pardon, sir." The dapper clerk bowed and hurrying to his desk took up a letter. "Mr. Rochester left this for you, Mr. Kent, before his departure last night."

"His departure!" Kent deposited his suit-case on one of the chairs and tore open the envelope. The note was a scrawl, which he had some difficulty in deciphering.

"Dear Kent," it ran. "Am called out of town; will be back Saturday. Saunders gave me some of his cheek this afternoon, so I fired him. I engaged John Sylvester to fill his place, who comes highly recommended. He will report for work to-morrow. Ta-ta--PHIL."

Kent thrust the note into his pocket and picked up his suit-case.

"Mr. Rochester states that he has engaged you," he said. "Your references--?"

"Here, sir." The clerk handed him a folded paper, and Kent ran his eyes down the sheet from the sentence: "To whom it may concern" to the signature, Clark Hildebrand. The statement spoke in high terms of John Sylvester, confidential clerk.

"I can refer you to my other employers, Mr. Kent," Sylvester volunteered as the young lawyer stood regarding the paper. "If you, desire further information there is Mr. Clymer and--"

"No, Judge Hildebrand's recommendation is sufficient." And at Kent's smile the clerk's anxious expression vanished. "Did Mr. Rochester give you any outline of the work?"

"Yes, sir; he told me to file the papers in the Hitchcock case, and attend to the morning correspondence."

"Very good. Has any one called this morning?"

"No, sir. These letters were addressed to you personally, and I have not opened them," Sylvester handed a neatly arranged package to Kent. "These," indicating several letters lying open on his desk, "are to the firm."

"Bring them to me in half an hour," and Kent walked into his private office, carefully closing the door behind him. Opening his suit-case he took out his brief bag and laid it on the desk in front of him together with the package of letters. Instead of opening the letters immediately, he tilted back in his chair and regarded the opposite wall in deep thought. Philip Rochester could not have selected a worse time to absent himself; three important cases were on the calendar for immediate trial and much depended on the firm's successful handling of them. Kent swore softly under his breath; his last warning to Rochester, that he would dissolve their partnership if the older man continued to neglect his practice, had been given only a month before and upon Kent's return from eight months' service in the Judge Advocate General's Department in France. Apparently his warning had fallen on deaf ears and Rochester was indulging in another periodic spree, for so Kent concluded, recalling the unsteady penmanship of the note handed to him by the new clerk, John Sylvester.

Kent was still frowning at the opposite wall when a faint knock sounded, and at his call Sylvester entered.

"Here are the letters received this morning, sir, and type-written copies of the answers to yesterday's correspondence which Mr. Rochester dictated before leaving," Sylvester explained as he placed the papers on Kent's desk. "If you will o.k. them, I will mail them at once."

Kent went through the letters with care, and the new clerk rose in his estimation as he read the excellent dictation of the clearly typed answers.

"These will do admirably," he announced. "Sit down and I will reply to the other letters."

At the end of an hour Sylvester closed his stenographic note book and collected the correspondence, by that time scattered over Kent's desk.

"I'll have these notes ready for your signature before lunch," he said as he picked up a newspaper from the floor where it had tumbled during Kent's search for some particular letter heads. "I brought in the morning paper, sir; thought perhaps you had not seen it."

"Thanks." Kent swung his chair nearer the window and opened the newspaper. He had purchased a copy when walking through Union Station on his arrival, but had left it in the cafeteria where he had snatched a cup of coffee and hot rolls before hurrying to his office.

He read a column devoted to international affairs, scanned an account of a senatorial wrangle, and was about to turn to the second page, whistling cheerily, when his attention was arrested by the headings:

> BANK CASHIER DIES IN POLICE COURT
> JAMES TURNBULL, MISTAKEN FOR BURGLAR,
> SUFFERS FATAL ATTACK OF ANGINA PECTORIS

Kent's whistle stopped abruptly, and clutching the paper in both hands, he devoured the short account printed under the scare heads:

> "While masquerading as a burglar on a wager,
> James Turnbull, cashier of the Metropolis Trust
> Company, was arrested by Officer O'Ryan at an
> early hour yesterday morning in the residence of
> Colonel Charles McIntyre.

> "Officer O'Ryan conducted his prisoner to the
> 8th Precinct Police Station, and later he was
> arraigned in the police court. The Misses

McIntyre appeared in person to prefer the
charges against the supposed burglar, who, on
being sworn, gave the name of John Smith.

"Philip Rochester, the well known criminal
lawyer, was assigned by the court to defend the
prisoner. Upon the evidence submitted Judge
Mackall held the prisoner for trial by the grand
jury.

"It was just after the Judge's announcement
that 'John Smith,' then sitting in the prisoners
cage, was seized with the attack of angina pectoris
which ended so fatally a few minutes later.
It was not until after he had expired that those
rendering him medical assistance became aware
that he was James Turnbull in disguise.

"James Turnbull was a native of Washington,
his father, the late Hon Josiah Turnbull of
Connecticut, having made this city his permanent
home in the early '90s. Mr. Turnbull was looked
upon as one of the rising young men in banking
circles; he was also prominent socially, was a
member of the Alibi, Metropolitan, and Country
Clubs, and until recently was active in all forms
of athletics, when his ill-health precluded active
exercise.

"Officer O'Ryan, who was greatly shocked by
the fatal termination to Mr. Turnbull's rash
wager, stated to the representatives of the press
that Mr. Turnbull gave no hint of his identity

while being interrogated at the 8th Precinct Station. Friends attribute Mr. Turnbull's disinclination to reveal himself to the court, to his enjoyment of a practical joke, not realizing that the resultant excitement of the scene would react on his weak heart.

"Mr. Turnbull is survived by a great aunt; he had no nearer relatives living. It is a singular coincidence that the lawyer appointed by the court to defend Turnbull was his intimate friend, Philip Rochester, who made his home with the deceased."

Kent read the column over and over, then, letting the paper slip to the floor, sat back in his chair, too dumb-founded for words. Jimmie Turnbull arrested as a burglar in the home of the girl he loved on charges preferred by her, and defended in court by his intimate friend, both of whom were unaware of his identity! Kent rumpled his fair hair until it stood upright. And Jimmie's death had followed almost immediately as the result of over-excitement!

Kent's eyes grew moist; he had been very fond of the eccentric, lovable bank cashier, whose knack of performing many a kindly act, unsolicited, had endeared him to friends and acquaintances alike. Kent had seen much of him after his return from France, for Jimmie's attention to Helen McIntyre had been only second to Kent's devotion to the latter's sister, Barbara. The two men had one bond in common. Colonel McIntyre disliked them and discouraged their calling, to the secret fury of both, but love had found a way--Kent's eyes kindled at the recollection of Barbara's half-shy, wholly tender reception of his ardent pleading.

Turnbull's courtship had met with a set-back where he had least expected it--Philip Rochester had fallen deeply in love with Helen and, encouraged by her father, had pressed his suit with ardor. Frequent quarrels between the two close friends had been the outcome, and Jimmie had confided to Kent, before the latter left on the business trip to Chicago from which he had returned that morning, that the situation had become intolerable and he had notified Rochester that he would no longer share his apartment with him, and to look for other quarters as quickly as possible.

So buried was Kent in his thoughts that he never heard Sylvester's knock, and it was not until the clerk stood at his elbow that he awoke from his absorption.

"A lady to see you, Mr. Kent," he announced. "Shall I show her in?"

"Certainly--her name?"

"She gave none." Sylvester paused on his way back to the door. "It is one of the Misses McIntyre."

"Good Lord!" Kent was on his feet, straightening his tie and brushing his rumpled hair. "Here, wait a minute"--clutching a whisk broom in a frantic endeavor to remove some of the signs of travel which still clung to him. But he had only opportunity for one dab at his left shoulder before Barbara entered the office. All else forgotten, Kent tossed down the whisk broom and the next instant he had clasped her hand in both of his, his eyes telling more eloquently than his stumbling words, his joy at seeing her again.

"This is a business call," she stated demurely, "on you and Mr. Rochester." Her lovely eyes held a glint of mischief as she mentioned Kent's partner, then her expression grew serious. "I want legal advice."

"I am afraid you will have to put up with me," Kent moved his chair closer to the one she had selected by the desk. "Rochester is out of town."

"What!" Barbara sat bolt upright. "Where--where's he gone?"

"I don't know"--Kent pulled Rochester's letter out of his pocket and re-read it. "He did not mention where he was going."

Barbara stared at him; she had paled.

"When did Philip leave?"

"Last night, I presume." Kent tipped back his chair and pressed a buzzer; a second later Sylvester appeared in the doorway.

"Did Mr. Rochester tell you where he was going?" he asked the clerk.

"No, sir. Mr. Rochester stated that you had his address.

"I?" Kent concealed his growing surprise. "Did he leave any message for me, other than the letter?"

"No, sir.

"At what hour did he leave the office?"

"I can't say, sir; he was still here when I went away at five o'clock. He gave me a key to the office so that I could get in this morning." Kent remained silent, and he added, "Is that all, sir?"

"Yes, thanks," and the clerk retired.

As the door closed Barbara turned to Kent. "Have you heard about Jimmie Turnbull?"

Her voice was a bit breathless as she put the question, but Kent, puzzling over his partner's eccentric conduct, hardly noted her agitation.

"Yes. I saw the account just now in the morning paper," he answered. "A shocking affair. Poor Turnbull! He was a good fellow."

"He was!" Barbara spoke with unaccustomed vehemence, and looking at her Kent saw that her eyes were filled with tears. Impulsively he threw his arm about her, holding her close.

"My heart's dearest," he murmured fondly. "If there is anything--anything I can do--"

Barbara straightened up and winked away the tears. "There is," she said tersely. "Investigate Jimmie's death."

Kent gazed at her in astonishment. "Please explain," he suggested. "The morning paper states very plainly that the cause of death was an attack of angina pectoris."

"Yes, I know, and that is what Philip Rochester contends also." Barbara paused and glanced about the office; they had the room to themselves. "B-but Helen believes otherwise."

Kent drew back. "What do you mean, Babs?" he demanded.

"Just that," Barbara spoke wearily, and Kent, giving her close attention, grew aware of dark shadows under her eyes which told plainly of a sleepless night. "I want to engage you as our counsel to help Helen find out about Jimmie's death."

"Find out what?" asked Kent, his bewilderment increasing. "Do you mean that Jimmie's death was not the result of a dangerous heart disease, but of foul play?"

Barbara nodded her head vigorously. "Yes."

Kent sat back in his chair and regarded her in silence for a second. "How could that be, Babs, in an open police court with dozens of spectators all about?" he asked.

"The slightest attempt to kill him would have been frustrated by the police officials; remember, a prisoner especially, is hedged in and guarded."

"Well, he wasn't so very hedged in," retorted Barbara. "I was there and saw how closely people approached Jimmie."

"Did you observe any one hand him anything?"

"N-no," Barbara drawled the word as she strove to visualize the scene in the court room; then catching Kent's look of doubt she added with unmistakable emphasis. "Helen and I do not believe that Jimmie died from natural causes; we think the tragedy should be investigated." Her soft voice deepened. "I must know the truth, Harry, dear; for I feel that perhaps I am responsible for Jimmie's death."

"You!" Kent's voice rose in indignant protest. "Absurd!"

"No, it isn't If it had not been for my wager with Jimmie, he never would have entered our house disguised as a burglar."

"What brought about the wager?"

"Last Sunday Helen was boasting of her two new police dogs which Philip Rochester recently gave her, and said how safe she felt. We've had several burglaries in our neighborhood," Barbara explained, "and when Jimmie scoffed at the dogs, I bet him that he could not break into the house without the dogs arousing the household. I never once thought about Jimmie's heart trouble," she confessed, and her lips quivered. "I feel so guilty."

"You are inconsistent, Babs," chided Kent gently. "One moment you reproach yourself for being the cause of bringing on Jimmie's heart attack, and the next you declare you believe he died through foul play. You," looking at her tenderly, while a whimsical smile softened his stern mouth, "don't go so far as to claim you murdered him, do you?"

"Of course I didn't!" Barbara spoke with indignant emphasis, and her fingers snapped in uncontrollable nervousness. "Jimmie was very dear"--she hesitated--"to us. Neither Helen nor I can leave a stone unturned until we know without a shadow of a doubt what killed him."

"That is easily proven," declared Kent. "An autopsy--"

"Helen asked the coroner to hold one."

Kent stared--the twins were certainly in earnest.

"My advice to you is to wait until you hear the result of the post-mortem from

Coroner Penfield," he said gravely. "Until we know definitely what killed Jimmie, speculation is idle."

Barbara rose at once. "I thought you would be more sympathetic," she remarked, and her voice was a bit unsteady. "I am sorry to have troubled you."

In an instant Kent was by her side. "Barbara," he entreated. "I promise solemnly to aid you in every possible way. My only happiness is in serving you," his voice was very tender. "I slave here day in and day out that I may sometime be able to make a home for you. Don't leave me in anger."

"I was not angry, only deeply hurt," Barbara confessed. "I have so longed to see you. I--I needed you! I--" The rest was lost as she bowed her head against Kent's broad shoulder, and his impassioned whispers of devotion brought solace to her troubled spirit.

"I must go," declared Barbara ten minutes later. "Father would make a fearful scene if he knew I had been here to see you." She picked up her hand-bag, preparatory to leaving. "Then I can tell Helen that you will aid us?"

"Yes." Kent stopped on his way to the door. "I will try and see the coroner this afternoon. In the meantime, Babs, can't you tell me what makes you suspect that Jimmie might have been killed?"

"I have nothing tangible to go on," she admitted. "Only a woman's instinct--"

Kent did not smile. "Instinct," he repeated thoughtfully. "Well, does your instinct hazard a guess as to the weapon, the opportunity, and the motive for such a crime? Jimmie Turnbull hadn't an enemy in the world."

Barbara looked at him oddly. "Suppose you find the answer to those conundrums," she suggested. "Don't come to the elevator; Margaret Brewster may see you with me, and she would tell father of our meeting."

"Is Mrs. Brewster still with you?" asked Kent, paying no attention to her protests as he accompanied her down the corridor. "I understood she planned to return to the West last week."

"She did, but father persuaded her to prolong her visit," Barbara was guilty of a grimace, then hailing the descending elevator she bolted into it and waved her good-by to Kent as the cage shot downward.

When Kent reentered his office he found Sylvester hanging up the telephone receiver.

"Mr. Clymer has telephoned to ask if you will come to the Metropolis Trust Company at once," he said, and before Kent could frame a reply he had darted into the coat closet and brought out his hat and cane, and handed them to him.

"Don't wait for me, but go out for your luncheon," directed Kent, observing the hour. "I have my key and can get in when I return if you should not be here," and not waiting to hear Sylvester's thanks, he hurried away.

The clock over the bank had just struck noon when Kent reached the fine office building which housed the Metropolis Trust Company, and as he entered the bank, a messenger stopped him.

"Mr. Clymer is waiting for you in his private office, sir," he said, and led the way past the long rows of mahogany counters and plate glass windows to the back of the bank, finally stopping before a door bearing the name, in modest lettering-- BENJAMIN AUGUSTUS CLYMER. The bank president was sensitive on one point; he never permitted initials only to be used before his name. The messenger's deferential knock was answered by a gruff command to enter. Clymer welcomed Kent with an air of relief.

"You know Colonel McIntyre," he said by way of introduction, and Kent became aware that the tall man lounging with his back to him in one of the leather covered chairs was Barbara's father. Colonel McIntyre returned Kent's bow with a curt nod, and then Clymer pushed forward a chair.

"Sit down, Kent," he began. "You have already handled several confidential affairs for the bank in a satisfactory manner, and I have sent for you to-day to ask your aid in an urgent matter. Before I go further I must ask you to treat what I am about to say as strictly confidential."

"Certainly, Mr. Clymer."

"Good! Then draw up your chair." Clymer waited until Kent had complied with his request. "You have heard of Jimmie Turnbull's sudden and tragic death?"

"Yes."

"As you know, he was cashier of this bank." Clymer spoke with deliberation. "Soon after word reached here of his death, the vice-president and treasurer of the bank had a careful examination made of his books and accounts." Clymer paused to clear his throat; he was troubled with an irritating cough. "Turnbull's accounts were found in first class order."

"I am sure they would be, Mr. Clymer," exclaimed Kent warmly. "Any one who knew Jimmie would never doubt his honesty."

McIntyre turned in his chair and regarded the speaker with no friendly eye, but aside from that, took no part in the conversation. Clymer did not at once resume speaking.

"To-day," he commenced finally, "Colonel McIntyre called at the bank and asked the treasurer, Mr. Gilmore, for certain valuable negotiable securities which he left in the bank's care a month ago. Mr. Gilmore told Colonel McIntyre that these securities had been given to Jimmie Turnbull last Saturday on his presentation of a letter from McIntyre requesting that they be turned over to the bank's cashier. McIntyre expressed his surprise and asked to see the letter "--Clymer paused and took a paper from his desk. "Here is the letter."

Kent took the paper and examined it closely.

"This is perfectly in order," he said. "A clear statement in Colonel McIntyre's handwriting and on his stationery."

For the first time Colonel McIntyre addressed him.

"The letter is in order," he acknowledged, "and written on my stationery, but it was not written by me. The letter is a clever forgery."

CHAPTER V. THE VANISHING MAN

It still lacked twenty minutes of nine o'clock that night when Harry Kent turned into the Saratoga apartment hotel, and not waiting to take one of the elevators, ran up the staircase to the apartment which had been occupied jointly by Jimmie Turnbull and Philip Rochester. Kent had already selected the right key from among those on the bunch he had found in Rochester's desk at the office, and slipping it into the key-hole of the outer door, he turned the lock and walked noiselessly inside the dark apartment.

The soft click of the outer door as it swung to was hardly noticeable, and Kent, pausing only long enough to get his breath from his run up the staircase, stepped into the living room and reached for the electric light switch. Instead of encountering the cold metal of the switch his groping fingers closed over warm flesh.

Startled as he was, Kent retained enough presence of mind to grasp the hand tightly; the next second a man hurled himself upon him and he gave back. Furniture in the path of the struggling men was overturned as they fought in silent desperation. Kent would have given much for light. He strained his eyes to see his adversary, but the pitch darkness concealed all but the vaguest outline. As Kent got his second wind, confidence in his strength returned and he redoubled his efforts; suddenly his hands shifted their grip and he swung his adversary backward, pinning him against the wall.

A faint, sobbing breath escaped the man, and Kent felt the whole figure against which he pressed, quiver and relax; the taut muscles of chest and arms grew slack, collapsed.

Kent stood in wonderment, peering ahead, his hands empty--the man had vanished!

Drawing a long, long breath Kent felt his way back to the electric switch and pressed the button, lighting both the wall brackets and the table lamps With both hands on his throbbing temples he gazed at the over-turned chairs; they, as well as his aching throat, testified to his encounter having been a reality and not a fantastic dream. His glance traveled this way and that about the room and rested longest on the opposite side of the room where he had pinned the man to the wall. Wall--! Kent leaned against a tall highboy and laughed weakly, immoderately. He had pushed the man straight against the door leading into Rochester's bedroom, and not, as he had supposed, against the solid wall.

The man had been quick-witted enough to grasp the situation; his pretended weakness had caused Kent to relax his hold, a turn of the knob of the door, which swung inward, and he had made his escape into the bedroom, leaving Kent staring into dark, empty space.

Gathering his wits together Kent hurried into the bedroom--it was empty; so also was the bathroom opening from it. From there Kent made the rounds of the apartment, switching on the light until the place was ablaze, but in spite of his minute search of closets and under beds and behind furniture he could find no trace of his late adversary. Kent stopped long enough in the pantry to refresh himself with a glass of water, then he returned to the living room and sat down in an arm chair by the window. He wanted time to think.

How had the man vanished so utterly, leaving no trace behind in the apartment? The window in Rochester's room was locked on the inside; in fact, all the apartment windows were securely fastened, he had found on his tour of inspection; the only one not locked was the oval, swinging window high up in the side wall of the bathroom; only a child could squeeze through it, Kent decided. The window looked into a well formed by the wings of the apartment house, and had a sheer drop of fifty feet to the ground below.

But for his unfortunate luck in backing the man against the bedroom door instead of the wall he would not have escaped, but how had the man realized so instantly that he was against a door in the pitch darkness? It certainly showed familiarity with his surroundings. Kent sat upright as an idea flashed through his brain--was the man Philip Rochester?

Kent scouted the idea but it persisted. Suppose it had been Philip Rochester awakened from a drunken slumber by his entrance in the dark; if so, nothing more likely than that he had mistaken him, Kent, for a burglar and sprung at him. But why had he disappeared without revealing his identity to Kent? Surely the same reason worked both ways--the man who had wrestled with him was as unaware of Kent's identity as Kent was of his--they had fought in the dark and in silence.

Kent laughed aloud. The situation had its amusing side; then, as recollection came of the scene in the bank that morning, his mirth changed to grim seriousness. At his earnest solicitation and backed by Benjamin Clymer's endorsement of his plan, Colonel McIntyre had agreed to give him until Saturday night to locate the missing securities; if he failed, then the colonel proposed placing the affair in the hands of the authorities.

Kent's firm mouth settled into dogged lines at the thought; such a procedure meant besmirching Jimmie Turnbull's name; let the public get the slightest inkling that the bank cashier was suspected of forgery and there would be the devil to pay. Kent was determined to protect the honor of his dead friend, and to aid Helen McIntyre in her investigation of his sudden death.

Jimmie Turnbull had been the soul of honor; that he had ever stooped to forgery was unbelievable. There was some explanation favorable to him--there must be. Kent's clenched fist struck the arm of his, chair a vigorous blow and he leapt to his feet. Wasting no further time on speculation, he commenced a systematic search of the apartment, replacing each chair and table as well as the rugs which had been over-turned in his recent tussle, after which he tried the drawers of Jimmie's desk. They were unlocked. A careful search brought nothing to light but receipted bills, some loose change, old dinner cards, theater programs, tea invitations, and several packages of cigarettes.

Turning from the desk Kent walked over to the table which he knew was Philip Rochester's property; he recalled having once seen Jimmie place some papers there by mistake; having done so once, the mistake might have occurred again. Taking out his partner's bunch of keys, he soon found one that fitted and opened the drawers. He had half completed his task, without finding any clew to the missing securities, when he was interrupted by the sound of the opening of the front door, and had but time to slam the drawers shut and pocket the keys when the night clerk of the hotel stepped inside the apartment and, closely followed by a sandy-haired man, walked into the living room. He halted abruptly at sight of Kent.

"Good evening, Mr. Kent," he exclaimed, and took in at a glance the orderly arrangement of the room. "Pardon my unceremonious entrance, but I had no idea you were here, sir; we received a telephone message that a burglar had broken in here."

"You did!" Kent stared at him. Was he right, after all, in his conjecture; had the man been Philip Rochester? It would seem so, for who else, after taking refuge elsewhere, would have telephoned a warning of burglars to the hotel office? "Have you any idea who sent the message, Mr. Stuart?"

"I have not; it was an out-side call--" Stuart turned to his companion. "Sorry I brought you here on an idiotic chase, Mr. Ferguson."

"That's all right," responded the detective good naturedly. "Would you like me to look through the apartment just to see if any one really is concealed on the premises, Mr. Kent?" he asked, and added quickly, seeing Kent hesitate, "I am from the central office; Mr. Stuart can vouch for me."

Kent's hesitation vanished. "I'd be obliged if you would, Ferguson." As he spoke he led the way to Rochester's bedroom. "Come with us, Stuart," as the clerk loitered behind.

"Guess not, sir; I'm needed down at the desk, we are short-handed to-night. Let me know how the hunt turns out," and he stepped into the vestibule. "Good night."

"Good night," called Kent, and he accompanied Ferguson as far as the bathroom door, then returned to his inspection of Rochester's table. He had just completed his task when the detective rejoined him.

"No trace of any one," the latter announced. "Some one put up a joke on Stuart, I imagine. Find what you wished, sir?"

Kent was distinctly annoyed by the question. "Yes," he replied shortly.

Ferguson ignored his curt tone. "Will you spare me a few minutes of your time, Mr. Kent?" he asked persuasively. "I won't detain you long."

"Certainly." Kent moved over to the chair in the window which he had occupied before and pointed to another, equally as comfortable.

"What can I do for you?" he asked as Ferguson dropped back and stretched himself in the soft depths of the big chair.

"Supply some information," answered the detective promptly. "Just a minute," as Kent started to interrupt. "You don't recall me, but I met you while working on the Chase case; you handled that trial in great shape," Ferguson looked admiringly at his companion. "Lots of the praise went to your partner, Mr. Rochester, but I know you did the work. Now, please let me finish," holding up a protesting hand. "I know you've carried Mr. Rochester in your firm; he's dead wood." Kent was silent. What the detective said was only too true. Rochester, realizing the talent and industry which characterized his younger partner, had withdrawn more and more from active practice, and had devoted himself to the social life of the National Capital.

"This is rather a long-winded way of reaching my point," finished the detective. "But, Mr. Kent, I want your assistance in a puzzling case."

"Go on, I'm listening." As he spoke, Kent drew out his cigar case and handed it to Ferguson. "The matches are on the smoking stand at your elbow. Now, what is it, Ferguson?"

His companion did not reply at once; instead he puffed at his cigar.

"Did you read in the paper about Mr. Turnbull's death?" he asked when the cigar was drawing to his satisfaction, and as Kent nodded a silent affirmative in answer to his question, he asked another. "Did you know him well?"

"Yes."

"Did he have an enemy?"

"Not to my knowledge." Kent was watching the detective narrowly; what was he driving at? "On the contrary Turnbull was extremely popular."

"With Colonel McIntyre?" Ferguson had hoped to surprise Kent with the question, but his companion's expression did not alter.

"N-no, perhaps he was not over-popular with the colonel," he admitted slowly. "What prompts the question, Ferguson?"

The detective hitched his chair nearer. "I'm going to lay all my cards on the table," he announced. "I need advice and you are the man to give it to me. Listen, Mr. Kent, this Jimmie Turnbull masquerades as a burglar night before last at the McIntyre house, is arrested, a charge brought against him for house-breaking by Miss Helen McIntyre, and shortly after he dies--"

"From angina pectoris," finished Kent, as the detective paused.

"So Mr. Rochester contended," admitted Ferguson. "We'll let that go for a minute. Now, when Miss McIntyre saw Turnbull's body, she demanded an autopsy. Why?"

"To discover the cause of death," answered Kent quietly. "That is obvious, Ferguson."

"Sure. And why did she wish to discover it?" He waited a brief instant, then answered his own question. "Because Miss McIntyre did not agree with Rochester that Turnbull had died from angina pectoris--that is obvious, too. Now, what made her think that?"

"I am sure I don't know"--Kent's air of candor was unmistakable and Ferguson showed his disappointment.

"Hasn't Miss McIntyre been to see you?"

"No," was Kent's truthful answer; Barbara was the younger twin and her sister was therefore, "Miss McIntyre."

"You must recollect, Ferguson," he added, "that had Miss McIntyre called to see me about poor Turnbull, I would not have discussed the interview with any one, under any conditions."

"Certainly. I am not asking you to break any confidences; in fact," Ferguson smiled, "I must ask you to consider our conversation confidential. Now, Mr. Kent, does it not strike you as odd that apparently the only man in Washington who really disliked Turnbull was Colonel McIntyre, and it is his daughter who intimates that Turnbull's death was not due to natural causes?"

"Oh, pshaw!" Kent shrugged his shoulders. "You are taking an exaggerated view of the affair. Colonel McIntyre is an honorable upright American, and Turnbull was the same."

"People speak highly of both men," acknowledged the detective. "I saw Mr. Clymer, president of Turnbull's bank this afternoon, and he paid a fine tribute to his dead cashier."

Kent drew an inward sigh of relief. Benjamin Clymer had proved true blue; he had not permitted Colonel McIntyre's desire for immediate publicity and belief in Turnbull's guilt to shake his faith in his friend.

"You see, Ferguson, there is no motive for such a crime as you suggest," he remarked.

"Oh, for the motive,"--Ferguson rubbed his hands nervously together as he shot a look at his questioner; the latter's clear-cut features and manly bearing inspired confidence. "We know of no motive," he corrected.

"And we know of no crime having been perpetrated," rapped out Kent. "Come, man; don't hunt a mare's nest."

"Ah, but it isn't a mare's nest!" Ferguson remarked dryly.

Kent bent eagerly forward--"You have heard from the coroner--"

"Not yet," Ferguson jerked forward his chair until his knees touched Kent.

Had either man looked toward the window near which they were sitting, he would have seen a black shadow squatting ape-like on the window ledge. As Kent leaned over to relight his cigar, the face at the window vanished, to cautiously reappear a second later.

"The case piqued my interest," continued the detective after a pause. "And I made an investigation on my own hook. After the departure of the McIntyre twins and Coroner Penfield, I went back to the court room and poked around the prisoners' cage. There I found this." He took out of his pocket a small bundle and carefully unwrapped the oil-skin cover.

"A handkerchief?" questioned Kent as the detective did not unfold the white muslin, but held it with care.

"Yes. One of the prisoners in the cage told me Turnbull dropped it as Dr. Stone and the deputy marshal carried him into the ante-room. Smell anything?" Holding up the handkerchief.

"Yes." Kent wrinkled his nose and sniffed several times. "Smells like fruit."

Ferguson nodded. "Good guess; I noticed the odor and went at once to Dr. McLane. He told me the handkerchief was saturated with amyl nitrite."

"Amyl nitrite," repeated Kent reflectively. "It is given for angina pectoris."

"Yes. Well, in this case it was the remedy and not the disease which killed Turnbull," announced Ferguson triumphantly.

"Nonsense!" ejaculated Kent. "I happen to know that the capsules contain only three minims--I once heard Turnbull say so."

"True, but Turnbull got a lethal dose, all right; and he thought he was taking only the regular one. Devilishly ingenious on the part of the criminal, wasn't it?

"Yes. Have you detected the criminal?" Kent put the question with unmoved countenance, but with inward foreboding; the detective's mysterious manner was puzzling.

"Not yet, but I will," Ferguson hesitated. "The first thing was to establish that a crime had really been committed."

Kent bent down and sniffed again at the handkerchief to which a faint fruity aroma still clung.

"How did you discover that?" he asked.

"Dr. McLane and I took the handkerchief to a laboratory and the chemist found from the number of particles of capsules in the handkerchief, that at least two capsules--or double the usual dose--had been crushed by Turnbull and the fumes inhaled by him; with fatal results."

"Hold on," cautioned Kent. "In the flurry of the moment, Turnbull may have accidentally put two capsules in the handkerchief, meaning only to use one."

"Mr. Kent," the detective spoke impressively, "that wasn't Turnbull's handkerchief."

"Not his own handkerchief!" exclaimed Kent. "Then, are you sure that Turnbull used it?"

"Yes; that fact is established by reputable witnesses; Dr. Stone, Mr. Clymer, and the deputy marshal," Ferguson spoke with increasing earnestness. "That is a woman's handkerchief--look at it."

Ferguson laid the little bundle on the broad arm of Kent's chair and with infinite care folded back the edges of the handkerchief, revealing as he did so, the small particles of capsules still clinging to the linen. But Kent hardly observed the capsules, his entire attention being centered on one corner of the handkerchief, which had neatly embroidered on it the letter "B."

CHAPTER VI. STRAIGHT QUESTIONS AND CROOKED ANSWERS

Colonel McIntyre, with an angry gesture, threw down the newspaper he had been reading.

"Do you mean to say, Helen, that you decline to go to the supper to-night on account of the death of Jimmie 'Turnbull?" he asked.

"Yes, father."

McIntyre flushed a dark red; he was not accustomed to scenes with either of his daughters, and here was Helen flouting his authority and Barbara backing her up.

"It is quite time this pretense is dropped," he remarked stiffly. "You were not engaged to Jimmie--wait," as she attempted to interrupt him. "You told me the night of the burglary that he was nothing to you.'"

"I was mistaken," Helen's voice shook, she was very near to tears. "When I saw Jimmie lying there, dead"--she faltered, and her shoulders drooped forlornly--"the world stopped for me."

"Hysterical nonsense!" McIntyre was careful to avoid Barbara's eyes; her indignant snort had been indicative of her feelings. "Keep to your room, Helen, until you regain some common sense. It is as well our friends should not see you in your present frame of mind."

Helen regarded her father under lowered lids. "Very well," she said submissively and walked toward the door; on reaching it she paused, and spoke over her shoulder. "Don't try me too far, father."

McIntyre stared for a full minute at the doorway through which Helen took her departure.

"Well, what the--" He pulled himself up short in the middle of the ejaculation and turned to Barbara. "Go and get dressed," he directed. "We must leave here in twenty minutes."

"I am not going," she announced.

"Not going!" McIntyre frowned, then laughed abruptly. "Now, don't tell me you were engaged to Jimmie Turnbull, also."

"I think you are horrid!" Barbara's small foot came down with a vigorous stamp.

"Well, perhaps I am," her father admitted rather wearily. "Don't keep us waiting, Babs; the car will be here in less than twenty minutes."

"But, father, I prefer to stay at home."

"And I prefer to have you accompany us," retorted McIntyre. "Come, Barbara, we cannot be discourteous to Mrs. Brewster; she is our guest, and this supper is for her entertainment."

"Well, take her." Barbara was openly rebellious.

"Barbara!" His tone caused her to look at him in wonder; instead of the stern rebuke she expected, his voice was almost wheedling. "I cannot very well take Mrs. Brewster to a cafe at this hour without causing gossip."

"Oh, fiddle-sticks!" exclaimed Barbara. "I don't have to play chaperon for you two. Every one knows she is visiting us; what's there improper in your taking her out to supper? Why"--regarding him critically--"she's young enough to be your daughter!"

"Go to your room!" There was nothing wheedling about McIntyre at that instant; he was thoroughly incensed.

As Barbara sped out happy in having gained her way, she announced, as a parting shot, "If you can be nasty to Helen; father, I can be nasty, too."

Colonel McIntyre brought his fist down on a smoking table with such force that he scattered its contents over the floor. When he rose from picking up the debris, he found Mrs. Brewster at his elbow.

"Can I help?" she asked.

"No, thanks, everything is back in place." He pulled forward a chair for her. "If agreeable to you I will telephone Ben Clymer that we will stop for him and take him with us to the Caf St. Marks; or would you prefer some other man?"

"Oh, no." She threw her evening wrap across the sofa and sat down. "Are the girls ready?"

"They--they are indisposed, and won't be able to go to-night."

"What! Both girls?"

"Yes, both"--firmly, not, however, meeting her eyes.

"Hadn't I better stay with them?" she asked. "Have you telephoned or Dr. Stone?"

"There is no necessity for giving up our little spree," he declared cheerily. "The girls don't need a physician. They"--with meaning, "need a mother's care." He picked up her coronation scarf from the floor where it had slipped and laid it across her bare shoulders; the action was almost a caress. She made a lovely picture as she sat in the high-backed carved chair in her chic evening gown, and as her soft dark eyes met his ardent look, McIntyre felt the hot blood surge to his temples, and with quickened pulse he went to the telephone stand and gave Central a number.

Back in her chair Mrs. Brewster sat thoughtfully watching him. She had been an unobserved witness of the scene with Barbara, having entered the library in time to hear the girl's last remarks. It was not the first inkling that she had had of their disapproval of Colonel McIntyre's attentions to her, but it had hurt.

The widow had become acquainted with the twins when, traveling in Europe just before the outbreak of the World War, and had made the hasty trip back to this country in their company. Colonel McIntyre had planned to bring the twins, then at school in Paris, home himself, but business had kept him in the West and he had cabled to a spinster cousin to chaperon them on the trip across the Atlantic Ocean. Nor had he reached New York in time to see them disembark, and thus had missed meeting Mrs. Brewster, then in her first year of widowhood.

The friendship between the twins and Mrs. Brewster had been kept up through much correspondence, and the widow had finally promised, to come to Washington for their debut, visiting her cousins, Dr. and Mrs. Stone. The meeting had but cemented the friendship between them, and at the twins' urgent request, seconded with warmth by Colonel McIntyre, she had promised to spend the month of April at the McIntyre home.

The visit was nearly over. Mrs. Brewster sighed faintly. There were two courses open to her, immediate departure, or to continue to ignore the twins' strangely antagonistic behavior--the first course did not suit Mrs. Brewster's plans.

Barbara, who had left the library through one of its seven doors, had failed to see Mrs. Brewster by the slightest margin; she was intent only on being with Helen. The affection between the twins was very close; but while their facial resemblance was remarkable, their natures were totally dissimilar. Helen, the elder by twenty minutes, was studious, shy, and too much given to introspection; Barbara, on the contrary, was whimsical and practical by turns, with a great capacity for enjoyment. The twins had made their debut jointly on their eighteenth birthday, and while both were popular, Barbara had received the greater amount of attention.

Barbara tip-toed into the suite of rooms which the girls occupied over the library, expecting to find Helen lying on the lounge; instead, she found her writing busily at her desk. She tossed down her pen as her sister entered, and, taking up a blotter, carefully laid it across the page she had been writing.

"Thank heaven, I don't have to go to that supper party," Barbara announced, throwing herself full length on the lounge.

"So father gave it up," commented Helen. "I am glad."

"Gave up nothing," retorted her sister. "He and Margaret Brewster are going."

"What!" Helen was on her feet. "You let them go out alone together?"

"They can't be alone if they are together," answered Barbara practically. "Don't be silly, Helen."

Helen did not answer at once; she had grown singularly pale. Walking over to the window she glanced into the street. "The car hasn't come," she exclaimed, and consulted her wrist watch. "Hurry, Babs, you have just, time to dress and go with them."

"B-b-but I said I wouldn't go," stuttered Barbara, completely taken by surprise.

"No matter; tell father you have changed your mind." Helen held out her hand. "Come, to please me," and there was a world of wistful appeal in her hazel eyes which Barbara was unable to resist.

It was not until Barbara had completed her hasty toilet and a frantic dash downstairs in time to spring into the waiting limousine after Margaret Brewster, that she realized she had put on one of Helen's evening gowns and not her own.

Benjamin Clymer was standing in the vestibule of the Saratoga, where he made his home, when the McIntyre limousine drew up, and he did not keep them waiting, as Colonel McIntyre had predicted he would on the drive to Clymer's apart-ment house.

"The clerk gave me your message when I came in, McIntyre," he explained as the car drove off. "I called up your residence and Grimes said you were on the way here."

Barbara, tucked away in her corner of the limousine, listened to Mrs. Brewster's animated chatter with utter lack of interest; she wished most heartily that she had not been over-persuaded by her sister, and had remained at home. That her father had accepted her lame explanation and her presence in the party with unaffected pleasure had been plain. Mrs. Brewster, after a quiet inquiry regarding her health, had been less enthusiastic in her welcome. Barbara was just stifling a yawn when the limousine stopped at the entrance to the Caf St. Marks.

Inside the caf all was light and gaiety, and Barbara brightened perceptibly as the attentive head waiter ushered them to the table Colonel McIntyre had reserved earlier in the evening.

"It's a novel idea turning the old church into a caf," Barbara remarked to Ben-jamin Clymer. "A sort of casting bread upon the waters of famished Washington. I wonder if they ever turn water into wine?"

"No such luck," groaned Clymer dismally, looking with distaste at the spar-kling grape juice being poured into the erstwhile champagne goblet by his plate. "The caf is crowded to-night," and he gazed with interest about the room. Colonel McIntyre, who had loitered behind to speak to several friends at an adjacent table, took the unoccupied seat by Mrs. Brewster and was soon in animated conversation with the widow and Clymer; Barbara, her healthy appetite asserting itself, devoted her entire attention to the delicious delicacies placed before her. The arrival of the after-the-theater crowd awoke her from her abstraction, and she accepted Clymer's invitation to dance with alacrity. When they returned to the table she discovered that Margaret Brewster and her father had also joined the dancers.

Barbara watched them while keeping up a disjointed conversation with Cly-mer, whose absentminded remarks finally drew Barbara's attention, and she won-dered what had come over the generally entertaining banker. It was on the tip of her tongue to ask him the reason for his distrait manner when her thoughts were diverted by his next remark.

"Your father and Mrs. Brewster make a fine couple," he said. "Colonel McIntyre is the most distinguished looking man in the caf and Mrs. Brewster is a regular beauty."

Instead of replying Barbara turned in her seat and scanned her father as he and Mrs. Brewster passed them in the dance. Colonel McIntyre did not look his age of forty-seven years. His hair, prematurely gray, had a most attractive wave to it, and his erect and finely proportioned figure showed to advantage in his well-cut dress suit. Barbara's heart swelled with pride--her dear and handsome father! Then she transferred her regard to Margaret Brewster; she had been such a satisfactory friend--why oh, why did she wish to become her step-mother? The twins, with the unerring instinct of womanhood, had decided ten days before that Weller's warning to his son was timely--Mrs. Brewster was a most dangerous widow.

"How is your sister?" inquired Clymer, breaking the silence which had lasted nearly five minutes. He was never quite certain which twin he was talking to, and generally solved the problem by familiarizing himself with their mode of dress. The plan had not always worked as the twins had a bewildering habit of exchanging clothes, to the enjoyment of Barbara's mischief loving soul, and the mystification of their numerous admirers.

"She is rather blue and depressed," answered Barbara. "We are both feeling the reaction from the shock of Jimmie Turnbull's tragic death. You must forgive me if I am not good company to-night."

The arrival of the head waiter at their table interrupted Clymer's reply.

"This gentleman desires to speak to you a moment, Miss McIntyre," he said, and indicated a young man in a sack suit standing just back of him.

"I'm Parker of the Post," the reporter introduced himself with a bow which included Clymer. "May I sit down?" laying his hand on the back of Mrs. Brewster's vacant chair.

"Surely; and won't you have an ice?" Barbara's hospitable instincts were aroused. "Here, waiter--"

"No, thanks; I haven't time," protested Parker, slipping into the chair. "I just came from your house, Miss McIntyre; the butler said I might find you here, and as it was rather important, I took the liberty of introducing myself. We plan to run a story, featuring the dangers of masquerading in society, and of course it hinges on the death of Mr. Turnbull. I'm sorry"--he apologized as he saw Barbara wince. "I realize the topic is one to make you feel badly; but I promise to ask only few questions." His smile was very engaging and Barbara's resentment receded somewhat.

"What are they?" she asked.

"Did you recognize Mr. Turnbull in his burglar's make-up when you confronted him in the police court?" Parker drew out copy paper and a pencil, and waited for her reply. There was a pause.

"I did not recognize Mr. Turnbull in court," she stated finally. "His death was a frightful shock."

"Sure. It was to everybody," agreed Parker. "How about your sister, Miss Barbara; did she recognize him?"

"No." faintly.

Parker showed his disappointment; he was not eliciting much information. Abruptly he turned to Clymer, whose prominent position in the financial world made him a familiar figure to all Washingtonians.

"Weren't you present in the police court on Tuesday morning also?" Parker asked.

"Yes," Clymer modified the curt monosyllable by adding, "I helped Dr. Stone carry Turnbull out of the prisoners' cage and into the anteroom."

"And did you recognize your cashier?" demanded Parker. At the question Barbara set down her goblet of water without care for its perishable quality and looked with quick intentness at the banker.

"I recognized Mr. Turnbull when his wig was removed," answered Clymer, raising his head in time to catch Barbara's eyes gazing steadfastly at him. With a faint flush she turned her attention to the reporter.

"Mr. Turnbull's make-up must have been superfine," Parker remarked. "Just one more question. Can you tell me if Mr. Philip Rochester recognized his roommate when he was defending him in court?"

"No, I cannot," and observing Parker's blank expression, she added, "why don't you ask Mr. Rochester?"

"Because I can't locate him; he seems to have vanished off the face of the globe." The reporter rose. "You can't tell me where's he's gone, I suppose?"

"I haven't the faintest idea," answered Barbara truthfully. "I was at his office this--" she stopped abruptly on finding that Mrs. Brewster was standing just behind her. Had the widow by chance overheard her remark? If so, her father would probably learn of her visit to the office of Rochester and Kent that morning.

"Do I understand that Philip Rochester is out of town?" inquired Mrs. Brewster. "Why, I had an appointment with him to-morrow."

"He's gone and left no address that I can find," explained Parker. "Thank you, Miss McIntyre; good evening," and the busy reporter hurried away.

There was a curious expression in Mrs. Brewster's eyes, but she dropped her gaze on her finger bowl too quickly for Clymer to analyze its meaning.

"What can have taken Mr. Rochester out of town?" she asked. The question was not addressed to any one in particular, but Colonel McIntyre answered it, as he did most of the widow's remarks.

"Dry Washington," he explained. "It isn't the first trip Philip has made to Baltimore since the 'dry' law has been in force, eh, Clymer?"

"No, and it won't be his last," was the banker's response. "What's the matter, Miss McIntyre?" as Barbara pushed back her chair.

"I feel a little faint," she stammered. "The air here is--is stifling. If you don't mind, father, I'll take the car and drive home."

"I'll come with you," announced Mrs. Brewster, rising hurriedly; and as she turned solicitously to aid Barbara she caught Colonel McIntyre's admiring glance and his whispered thanks.

Outside the caf Clymer discovered that the McIntyre limousine was not to be found, and, cautioning Barbara and the widow to remain where they were, he went back into the caf in search of Colonel McIntyre, who had stayed behind to pay his bill.

A sudden exodus from the caf as other diners came out to get their cars, separated Barbara from Mrs. Brewster just as the former caught sight of her father's limousine coming around McPherson Square. Not waiting to see what had become of her companion, Barbara started up the sidewalk intent on catching their chauffeur's attention. As she stood by the curb, a figure brushed by her and a paper was deftly slipped inside her hand.

Barbara wheeled about abruptly. She stood alone, except for several elaborately dressed women and their companions some yards away who were indulging in noisy talk as they hurried along. At that moment the McIntyre limousine stopped at the curb and the chauffeur opened the door.

"Take me home, Harris," she ordered. "And then come back for Mrs. Brewster and father. I don't feel well--hurry."

"Very good, miss," and touching his cap the chauffeur swung his car up Fifteenth Street.

The limousine had turned into Massachusetts Avenue before Barbara switched on the electric lamp in the car and opened the note so mysteriously given to her. She read feverishly the few lines it contained,

> Dear Helen:
>   The coroner will call an inquest. Secrete letter "B."

The note was unsigned but it was in the handwriting of Philip Rochester.

CHAPTER VII. THE RED SEAL

The gloomy morning, with leaden skies and intermittent rain, reflected Harry Kent's state of mind. He could not fix his attention on the business letters which Sylvester placed before him; instead, his thoughts reverted to the scene in Rochester's and Turnbull's apartment the night before, the elusive visitor he had found there on his arrival, his interview with Detective Ferguson, and above all the handkerchief, saturated with amyl nitrite, and bearing the small embroidered letter "B"--the initial, insignificant in size, but fraught with dire possibilities if, as Ferguson hinted, Turnbull had been put to death by an over-dose of the drug. "B "--Barbara; Barbara--"B"--his mind rang the changes; pshaw! other names than Barbara began with "B."

"Shall I transcribe your notes, Mr. Kent?" asked Sylvester, and Kent awakened from his reverie, discovered that he had scrawled the name Barbara and capital "Bs" on the writing pad. He tore off the sheet and crumpled it into a small ball. "No, my notes are unimportant." Kent unlocked his desk and took some manuscript from one of the drawers. "Make four copies of this brief, then call up the printer and ask how soon he will complete the work on hand. Has Mr. Clymer telephoned?"

"Not this morning." Sylvester rose, papers in hand. "There has been a Mr. Parker of the Post who telephones regularly once an hour to ask for Mr. Rochester's address and when he is expected at the office." He paused and looked inquiringly at Kent. "What shall I say the next time he calls?"

"Switch him on my phone," briefly. "That is all now, Sylvester. I must be in court by noon, so have the brief copied by eleven."

"Yes, sir," and Sylvester departed, only to return a second later. "Miss McIntyre to see you," he announced, and stood aside to allow the girl to enter.

It was the first time Kent had seen Helen since the tragedy of Tuesday and as he advanced to greet her he noted with concern her air of distress and the troubled look in her eyes. Her composed manner was obviously only maintained by the exertion of self-control, for the hand she offered him was unsteady.

"You are so kind," she murmured as he placed a chair for her. "Babs told me you have promised your aid, and so I have come--" she pressed one hand to her side as if she found breathing difficult and Kent, reaching for his pitcher of ice water which stood near at hand, filled a tumbler and gave it to her.

"Take a little," he coaxed as she moved as if to refuse the glass. "Why didn't you telephone and I would have called on you; in fact, I planned to run in and see you this afternoon.

"It is wiser to have our talk here," she replied. Setting down the empty glass she gazed about the office and her face brightened at sight of a safe standing in one corner. "Is that yours or Philip's?" she asked, pointing to it.

"The safe? Oh, it's for our joint use, owned by the firm, you know," explained Kent, somewhat puzzled by her eagerness.

"Do you keep your private papers there, as well as the firm's?"

"Oh, yes; Philip has retained one section and I the other." Kent walked over and threw open the massive door which he had unlocked on entering the office and left ajar. "Would you like to see the arrangements of the compartments?"

Without answering Helen crossed the room and stood by his side.

"Which is Philip's section?" she asked.

"This," and Kent touched the side of the safe.

Helen turned around and inspected the office; the outer door through which she had entered was closed, as were also the private door leading directly into the outside corridor, and the one opening into the closet. Convinced that they were really alone, she took from her leather hand-bag a white envelope and handed it to Kent.

"Please put this in Philip's compartment," she said, and as he hesitated, she added pleadingly, "Please do it, Harry, and ask no questions."

Kent looked at her wonderingly; the girl was obviously laboring under intense excitement of some sort, which might at any moment break into hysteria. Bottling up his curiosity, he stooped down in front of the safe.

"Certainly I will put the envelope away for you," he agreed cheerily. "Wait, though, I must find if Philip left the key of the compartment on his bunch." He took from his pocket the keys he had found so useful the night before, and selected one that resembled the key to his own compartment, and inserted it in the lock. To his surprise he discovered the compartment was already unlocked. Without comment he pulled open the inside drawer and started to lay the white envelope on top of the papers already there, when he hesitated.

"The envelope is unaddressed, Helen," he remarked, extending it toward her. She waved it back.

"It is sealed with red wax," she stated. "That is all that is necessary for identification."

Kent turned over the envelope--the flap was held down securely with a large red seal which bore the one letter "B." He dropped the envelope inside the drawer, locked the compartment, and closed the door of the safe.

"Let us talk," he suggested and led the way back to their chairs. "Helen," he began, after she was seated. "There is nothing I will not do for your sister Barbara," his manner grew earnest. "I--" he flushed; baring his feelings to another, no matter how sympathetic that other was, was foreign to his reserved nature. "I love her beyond words to express. I tell you this to--to--gain your trust."

"You already have it, Harry!" Impulsively Helen extended her hand, and he held it in a firm clasp for a second. "Babs and I have come at once to you in our trouble."

"Yes, but you have only hinted what that trouble, was," he reminded her gently. "I cannot really aid you until you give me your full confidence."

Helen looked away from him and out of the window. The relief, which had lighted her face a moment before, had vanished. It was some minutes before she answered.

"Babs told you that I suspected Jimmie did not die from angina pectoris--" She spoke with an effort.

"Yes."

She waited a second before continuing her remarks. "I have asked the coroner to make an investigation." She paused again, then added with more animation, "He is the one to tell us if a crime has been committed."

"He can tell if death has been accelerated by a weapon, or a drug," responded Kent; he was weighing his words carefully so that she might understand him fully. "But to constitute a crime, it has to be proved first, that the act has been committed, and second, that a guilty mind or malice prompted it. Can you furnish a clew to establish either of the last mentioned facts in connection with Jimmie's death?"

Kent wondered if she had heard him, she was so long in replying, and he was about to repeat his question when she addressed him.

"Have you heard from Coroner Penfield?"

"No. I tried several times to get him on the telephone, but without success," replied Kent; his disappointment at not receiving an answer to his question showed in his manner. "I went to Penfield's house last night, but he had been called away on a case and, although I waited until nearly ten o'clock, he had not returned when I left. Have you had word from him?"

"Not--not directly." She had been nervously twisting her handkerchief about in her fingers; suddenly she turned and looked full at Kent, her eyes burning feverishly. "I would give all I possess, my hope of future happiness even, if I could prove that Jimmie died from angina pectoris."

Kent looked at her in mingled sympathy and doubt.--What did her words imply--further tragedy?

"Jimmie might not have died from angina pectoris," he said, "and still not have been poisoned--"

"You mean--"

"Suicide."

Slowly Helen took in his meaning, but she volunteered no remark, and Kent after a pause, added, "While I have not seen Coroner Penfield I did hear last night what killed Jimmie." Helen straightened up, one hand pressed to her heart. "It was a lethal dose of amyl nitrite."

"Amyl nitrite," she repeated. "Yes, I have heard that it is given for heart trouble. How"--she looked at him queerly. "How is it administered?"

"By crushing a capsule in a handkerchief and inhaling its fumes "--he was watching her closely. "The handkerchief Jimmie was seen to use just before he died was found to contain two or more broken capsules."

Helen sat immovable for over a minute, then she bowed her head and burst into dry tearless sobs which wracked her body. Kent laid a tender hand on her shoulder, then concluding it was better for her to have her cry out, he wandered aimlessly about the office waiting for her to regain her composure.

He stopped before one of the windows facing south and stared moodily at the Belasco Theater. That playhouse had surely never staged a more complicated mystery than the one he had set himself to unravel. What consolation could he offer Helen? If he encouraged her belief in his theory that Jimmie committed suicide he would have to establish a motive for suicide, and that motive might prove to be the theft of Colonel McIntyre's valuable securities. Threatened with exposure as a thief and forger, Jimmie had committed suicide, so would run the verdict; the fact of his suicide was proof of his guilt of the crime Colonel McIntyre virtually charged him with, and vice versa.

What had been discovered to point to murder? The finding of a handkerchief, saturated with amyl nitrite, which had not belonged to the dead man. Proof--bah! it was ridiculous! What more likely than that Jimmie, while in the McIntyre house before his arrest as a burglar, had picked up one of Barbara's handkerchiefs, stuffed it inside his pocket, and when threatened with exposure on being held for the grand jury, had, in desperation, crushed the amyl nitrite capsules in Barbara's handkerchief and killed himself.

Kent drew a long, long sigh. His faith in Jimmie's honesty was shaken at last by the accumulative evidence, and he was convinced that he had found the solution to the problem, but how impart it to the weeping girl? To prove her lover a thief, forger, and suicide was indeed a task he shrank from.

A ring at the telephone caused Kent to move hastily to the instrument; when he hung up the receiver Helen was adjusting her veil before a mirror over the mantel.

"Colonel McIntyre is in the next room," he said, keeping his voice lowered.

"My father!" Helen's eyes were hard and dry. "Does he know that I am here?"

"I don't know; Sylvester simply said he had called to see me and is waiting in the outer office." Observing her indecision, Kent opened the door leading directly into the corridor. "You can leave this way without encountering Colonel McIntyre."

Helen hurried through the door and paused in the corridor to whisper feverishly in Kent's ear, "Promise me you will remain faithful to Barbara whatever develops."

"I will!" Kent's pledge rang out clearly, and Helen with a lighter heart turned to walk away when a telegraph boy appeared around the corner of the corridor and thrust a yellow envelope at Kent, who stood half inside his office watching Helen.

"Sign here," the boy said, indicating the line on the receipt slip, and getting it back, departed.

Motioning to Helen to wait, Kent tore open the telegram. It was from Cleveland and dated the night before. The message ran: Called to Cleveland. Address City Club. Rochester.

Without comment Kent held out the telegram so that Helen could read it.

"What!" she exclaimed. "Philip in Cleveland last night. I--I--don't understand." And looking at her Kent was astounded at the flash of terror which shone for an instant in her eyes. Before he had time to question her she bolted around the corridor.

Kent remained staring ahead for an instant then returned thoughtfully to his office, and within a second Sylvester received a telephone message to show Colonel McIntyre into Kent's office. Not only Colonel McIntyre followed the clerk into the room but Benjamin Clymer. "Any further developments, Kent?" inquired the banker. "No, we can't sit down; just dropped in to see you a minute."

"There is nothing new," Kent had made instant decision; such information regarding the death of Turnbull as he had gleaned from Ferguson, and the events of the night before should be confided to Clymer alone, and not in the presence of Colonel McIntyre.

"Did you search Turnbull's apartment last night as you spoke of doing?" asked McIntyre.

"I did, and found no trace of your securities, Colonel."

McIntyre lifted his eyebrows as he smiled sarcastically. "Can I see Rochester?" he asked.

"He is in Cleveland; I don't know just when he will be back."

"Indeed? Too bad you haven't the benefit of his advice," remarked McIntyre insolently. "At Clymer's request, Kent, I have allowed you until Saturday night to find the securities and either clear Turnbull's name or admit his guilt; there remain two days and a half before I take the affair in my own hands and make it public."

"I hope to establish Turnbull's innocence before that time," retorted Kent coolly.

Inwardly his spirits sank; had not every effort on his part brought but further proof of Jimmie's guilt? That McIntyre would make no attempt to hush up the scandal was obvious.

"Keep me informed of your progress," McIntyre's manner was domineering and Kent felt the blood mount to his temples, but he was determined not to lose his temper whatever the provocation; McIntyre was Barbara's father.

Clymer, aware that the atmosphere was getting strained, diplomatically intervened.

"Dine with me to-night, Kent," he said. "Perhaps you will then have some news that will throw light on the present whereabouts of the securities. I found, on making inquiries, that they have not been offered for sale in the usual channels. Come, McIntyre, I have a directors' meeting in twenty minutes."

McIntyre, who had been swinging his walking stick from one hand to the other in marked impatience, turned to Kent, his manner more conciliatory.

"Pleasant quarters you have," he remarked. "Does Rochester share his room with you?"

"No, Colonel, his is across the ante-room where you waited a few minutes ago," explained Kent as he accompanied his visitors to the door. "This is my office."

"Ah, yes, I thought as much on seeing only one desk," McIntyre's manner grew more cordial. "Does Rochester's furniture duplicate yours, safe and all?"

"Safe--no, he has none; that is the firm's safe." Kent was becoming restless under so many personal questions. "Good-by, Mr. Clymer."

"Don't forget to-night at eight," the banker reminded him before stepping into the corridor. "We'll dine at the Club de Vingt. Come along, McIntyre."

Sylvester stopped Kent on his way back to his office and handed him the neatly typewritten copies of his brief, and with a word of thanks the lawyer went over to his desk and, gathering such papers as he required at the court house, he thrust them and the brief into his leather bag, but instead of hurrying on his way, he stood still to consider the events of the morning.

Helen McIntyre, during their interview, had not responded to his appeal for her confidence, nor vouchsafed any reason for her belief that Jimmie Turnbull had been the victim of foul play. And Colonel McIntyre had given him only until Saturday night to solve the problem! Kent's overwrought feelings found vent in an emphatic oath.

"Excuse me," exclaimed Sylvester mildly from the doorway. "I knocked and understood you to say come in.

"Well, what is it?" Kent's nerves were getting a bit raw; a glance at his watch showed him he had a slender margin only in which to reach the court house in time for his appointment. Not even waiting for the clerk's reply he snatched up his brief case and made for the private door leading into the corridor. But he was destined not to get away without another interruption.

As Sylvester was hastily explaining, "Two gentlemen to see you, Mr. Kent," the clerk was thrust aside and Detective Ferguson entered, accompanied by a deputy marshal.

"Sorry to detain you, Mr. Kent," exclaimed the detective. "I came to tell you that Coroner Penfield has just called an inquest for this afternoon to inquire into Jimmie Turnbull's death. Where's your partner, Mr. Rochester?" looking around inquiringly.

"In Cleveland. Won't I do?" replied Kent, his appointment forgotten in the news that Ferguson had just given him.

"No, we didn't come for legal advice," Ferguson smiled; then grew serious. "What's Mr. Rochester's address?"

Kent walked over to his desk and picked up the telegram. "The City Club, Cleveland," he stated.

"Thanks," Ferguson jotted down the address in his note-book. "Jones, here," placing his hand on his companion, "came to serve Mr. Rochester with a subpoena; he's wanted at the Turnbull inquest as a material witness."

CHAPTER VIII. THE INQUEST

Coroner Penfield adjusted his eyeglasses and scanned the spectators gathered for the Turnbull inquest. The room was crowded with both men and women, the latter predominating, and the coroner decided that, while some had come from a personal interest in the dead man, the majority had been attracted by morbid curiosity. There was a stir among the spectators as an inner door opened and the jury, led by the morgue master filed into the room and took their places. Coroner Penfield rose and addressed the foreman.

"Have you viewed the body?" he inquired.

"Yes, doctor," and the man sat down.

Coroner Penfield then concisely stated the reason for the inquest and summoned Officer O'Ryan to the witness stand. The policeman stood, cap in hand, while being sworn by the morgue master, and then took his place on the platform in the chair reserved for the witnesses.

His answer to Coroner Penfield's questions relative to his name, residence in Washington, and length of service in the city Police Force were given with brevity and a rich Irish brogue.

"Where were you on Tuesday morning at about five o'clock?" asked Penfield, first consulting some memoranda on his desk.

"On my way home," explained O'Ryan. "My relief had just come."

"Does your beat take in the McIntyre residence?"

"It does, sir."

"Did you observe any one loitering in the vicinity of the residence prior to five o'clock, Tuesday morning?"

"No, sir. It was only when the lady called to me that I was attracted to the house."

"Did she state what was the matter?"

"Yes, sir. She said that she had locked a burglar in a closet, and to come and get him, and I did so," and O'Ryan expanded his chest with an air of satisfaction as be glanced about the morgue.

"Did the burglar resist arrest?"

"No, sir; he came very peaceably and not a word out of him."

"Had you any idea that the burglar was not what he seemed?"

"Devil an idea, begging your pardon"--O'Ryan remembered hastily where he was. "The burglar looked the part he was masquerading, and his make-up was perfect," ended O'Ryan with relish. "Never gave me a hint he was a gentleman and a bank cashier in disguise."

Kent, who had arrived at the morgue a few minutes before the policeman commenced his testimony, smiled in spite of himself. He was feeling exceedingly low spirited, and had come to the inquest with inward foreboding as to its result. On what developed there, he Was convinced, hung Jimmie Turnbull's good name. After his interview with Detective Ferguson that morning, he had wired Philip Rochester to return to Washington at once. He had requested an immediate reply, and had fully expected to find a telegram at his office when he stopped there on his way to the morgue, but none had come.

"Whom did you see in the McIntyre house?" the coroner asked O'Ryan.

"No one sir, except the burglar and Miss McIntyre."

"Did you find any doors or windows unlocked?"

"No, sir; I never looked to see."

"Why not?"

"Because the young lady said that she had been over the house and everything was then fastened." O'Ryan looked anxiously at the coroner. Would he make him out derelict in his duty? It would seriously affect his standing on the Force. "I took Miss McIntyre's word for the house, for I had the burglar safe under arrest."

"How did Miss McIntyre appear?"

"Appear? Sure, she looked very sweet in her blue wrapper and her hair down her back," answered O'Ryan with emphasis.

"She was not fully dressed then?"

"No, sir."

"Was Miss McIntyre composed in manner or did she appear frightened?" asked

Penfield. It was one of the questions which Kent had expected, and he waited with intense interest for the policeman's reply.

"She was very pale and--and breathless like." O'Ryan flapped his arms about vaguely in his endeavor to demonstrate his meaning. "She kept begging me to hurry and get the burglar out of the house, and after telling her that she would have to appear in the Police Court first thing that morning, I went off with the prisoner."

"Were there lights in the house?" questioned Penfield.

"Only dim ones in the halls and two bulbs turned on in the library; it's a big room though, and they hardly made any light at all," explained O'Ryan; he was particular as to details. "I used handcuffs on the prisoner, thinking maybe he'd give me the slip in the dim light, but there was no fight or flight in him."

"Did he talk to you on the way to the station house?"

"No, sir; and at the station he was just as quiet, only answered the questions the desk sergeant put to him, and that was all," stated O' Ryan.

Penfield laid down his memorandum pad. "All right, O'Ryan; you may retire," and at the words the policeman left the platform and the room. He was followed by the police sergeant who had been on desk duty at the Eighth Precinct on Tuesday morning. His testimony simply corroborated O'Ryan's statement that the prisoner had done and said nothing which would indicate that he was other than he seemed--a housebreaker.

Coroner Penfield paused before calling the next witness and drank a glass of ice water; the weather had turned unseasonably hot, and the room in which inquests were held, was stifling, in spite of the long opened windows at either end.

"Call Miss Helen McIntyre," Penfield said to the morgue master, and the latter crossed to the door leading to the room where sat the witnesses. There was instant craning of necks to catch a glimpse of the society girl about whom, with her twin sister, so much interest centered.

Helen was extremely pale as she advanced up the room, but Kent, watching her closely, was relieved to see none of the nervousness which had been so marked at their interview that morning. She was dressed with fastidious taste, and as she mounted the platform after the morgue master had administered the oath, Coroner Penfield rose and, with a polite gesture, indicated the chair she was to occupy.

"I am Helen McIntyre," she announced clearly. "Daughter of Colonel Charles

McIntyre."

"Tell us the circumstances attending the arrest of James Turnbull, alias John Smith, in your house on Tuesday morning, Miss McIntyre," directed the coroner, seating himself at his table, on which were writing materials.

"I was sitting up to let in my sister, who had gone to a dance," she began, "and fearing I would fall asleep I went down into the library, intending to sit in one of the window recesses and watch for her arrival. As I entered the library I saw a figure steal across the room and disappear inside a closet. I was very frightened, but had sense enough left to cross softly to the closet and lock the door." She paused in her rapid recital and drew a long breath, then continued more slowly:

"I hurried to the window and across the street I saw a policeman standing under a lamp-post. It took but a minute to call him. The policeman opened the closet door, put handcuffs on Mr. Turnbull and took him away."

Coroner Penfield, as well as the jurors, followed her statement with absorbed attention. At its end he threw down his pencil and spoke briefly to the deputy coroner, who had been busily engaged in taking notes of the inquest, and then he turned to Helen.

"You heard no sound before entering the library?"

"No one walking about the house?" he persisted.

"No." She followed the negative with a short explanation. "I lay down on my bed soon after dinner, not feeling very well, and slept through the early hours of the night."

"At what hour did you wake up?"

"About four o'clock, or a little after."

"Then you were awake an hour before you discovered the supposed burglar in your library?"

"Y-yes," Helen's hesitation was faint. "About that length of time."

"And you heard no unusual sounds in that hour's interval?"

"I heard nothing"--her manner was slightly defiant and Kent's heart sank; if he had only thought to warn her not to antagonize the coroner.

"Where were you during that hour?"

"Lying down," promptly. "Then, afraid I would drop off to sleep again, I went downstairs."

Coroner Penfield consulted his notes before asking another question.

"Who lives in your house beside you and your twin sister?" he asked.

"My father, Colonel McIntyre; our house guest, Mrs. Louis C. Brewster, and five servants," she replied. "Grimes, the butler; Martha, our maid; Jane, the chambermaid; Hope, our cook; and Thomas, our second man; the chauffeur, Harris, the scullery maid, and the laundress do not stay at night."

"Who were at home beside yourself on Monday night and early Tuesday morning?"

"My father and Mrs. Brewster; I believe the servants were in also, except Thomas, who had asked permission to spend the night in Baltimore."

"Miss McIntyre?" Coroner Penfield put the next question in an impressive manner. "On discovering the burglar why did you not call your father?"

"My first impulse was to do so," she answered promptly. "But on leaving the library I passed the window, saw the policeman, and called him in." She shot a keen look at the coroner, and added softly, "The policeman was qualified to make an arrest; my father would have had to summon one had he been there."

"Quite true," acknowledged Penfield courteously. "Now, Miss McIntyre, why did the prisoner so obligingly walk straight into a closet on your arrival in the library?"

"I presume he was looking for a way out of the room and blundered into it," she explained. "There are seven doors opening from our library; the prisoner may have heard me approaching, become confused, and walked through the wrong door."

"That is quite plausible--with an ordinary bona-fide burglar," agreed Penfield. "But was not Mr. Turnbull acquainted with the architectural arrangements of your house?"

"He was a frequent caller and an intimate friend," she said, with dignity. "As to his power of observation and his bump of locality I cannot say. The library was but dimly lighted."

"Miss McIntyre," Penfield spoke slowly. "Were you aware of the real identity of the burglar?"

"I had no suspicion that he was not what he appeared," she responded. "He said or did nothing after his arrest to give me the slightest inkling of his identity."

Penfield raised his eyebrows and shot a look at the deputy coroner before going on with his examination.

"You knew Mr. Turnbull intimately, and yet you did not recognize him?" he asked.

"He wore an admirable disguise." Helen touched her lips with the tip of her tongue; inwardly she longed for the glass of ice water which she saw standing on the reporters' table. "Mr. Turnbull's associates will tell you that he excelled in amateur theatricals."

Penfield looked at her critically for a moment before continuing his questions. She bore his scrutiny with composure.

"Officer O'Ryan has testified that you informed him you examined the windows of your house," he said, after a brief wait. "Did you find any unlocked?"

"Yes; one was open in the little reception room off the front door."

"What floor is the room on?"

"The ground floor."

"Would it have been easy for any one to gain admittance through the window without attracting attention in the street?" was Penfield's next question.

"Yes."

"Miss McIntyre," Penfield rose, "I have only a few more questions to put to you. Why did Mr. Turnbull come to your house--a house where he was a welcome visitor--in the middle of the night disguised as a burglar?"

The reporters as well as the spectators bent forward to catch her reply.

"Mr. Turnbull had a wager with my sister, Barbara," she explained. "She bet him that he could not break into the house without being discovered."

Penfield considered her answer before addressing her again.

"Why didn't Mr. Turnbull tell you who he was when you had him arrested?" he asked.

Helen shrugged her shoulders. "I cannot answer that question, for I do not know his reason. If he had only confided in me"--her voice shook--"he might have been alive to-day."

"How so?" Penfield shot the question at her.

"Because then he would have been spared the additional excitement of his trip to the police station and the scene in court, which brought on his attack of angina pectoris."

Penfield regarded her for a moment in silence.

"I have no further questions, Miss McIntyre," he said, and turned to the morgue master. "Ask Miss Barbara McIntyre to come to the platform." Turning back to his table and the papers thereon he failed to see the twins pass each other in the aisle. They were identically attired and when Coroner Penfield looked again at the witness chair, he stared in surprise at its occupant.

"I beg pardon, Miss McIntyre, I desire your sister to testify," he remarked.

"I am Barbara McIntyre." A haunting quality in her voice caught Kent's attention, and he leaned eagerly forward, his eyes following each movement of her nervous fingers, busily twisting her gloves inside and out.

"I beg your pardon," exclaimed the coroner, recovering from his surprise. He had seen the twins at the police court on Tuesday morning for a second only, and then his attention had been entirely centered on Helen. He had heard, but had not realized until that moment, how striking was the resemblance between the sisters.

"Miss McIntyre," the coroner cleared his throat and commenced his examination. "Where were you on Monday night?"

"At a dance given by Mr. and Mrs. Charles Grosvenor."

"At what hour did you return?"

"I think it was half past five or a few minutes earlier."

"Who let you in?"

"My sister."

"Did you see the burglar?"

"He had left," she answered. "My sister told me of her adventure as we went upstairs to our rooms."

"Miss McIntyre," Penfield picked up a page of the deputy coroner's closely written notes, and ran his eyes down it. "Your sister has testified that James Turnbull went to your house disguised as a burglar on a wager with you. What were the terms of that wager?"

"I bet him that he could not enter the house after midnight without his presence being detected by our new police dogs," exclaimed Barbara slowly. She had stopped twirling her gloves about, and one hand was firmly clenched over the arm of her chair.

"Did the dogs discover his presence in the house?"

"Apparently not, or they would have aroused the household," she said. "I cannot answer that question, though, because I was not at home."

"Where are the dogs kept?"

"In the garage in the daytime."

"And at night?" he persisted.

"They roam about our house," she admitted, "or sleep in the boudoir, which is between my sister's bedroom and mine.

"Were the dogs in the house on Monday night?"

"I did not see them on my return from the dance."

"That is not an answer to my question, Miss McIntyre," the coroner pointed out. "Were the dogs in the house?"

There was a distinct pause before she spoke. "I recall hearing our butler, Grimes, say that he found the dogs in the cellar. Mr. Turnbull's shocking death put all else out of my mind; I never once thought of the dogs."

"In spite of the fact that it was a wager over the dogs which brought about the whole situation?" remarked the coroner dryly.

Barbara flushed at his tone, then grew pale.

"I honestly forgot about the dogs," she repeated. "Father sent them out to our country place Tuesday afternoon; they annoyed our--our guest, Mrs. Brewster."

"In what way?"

"By barking--'they are noisy dogs."

"And yet they did not arouse the household when Mr. Turnbull broke into the house"--Coroner Penfield regarded her sternly. "How do you account for that?"

Barbara's right hand stole to the arm of her chair and clasped it with the same convulsive strength that she clung to the other chair arm. When she spoke her voice was barely audible.

"I can account for it in two ways," she began. "If the dogs were accidentally locked in the cellar they could not possibly hear Mr. Turnbull moving about the house; if they were roaming about and scented him, they might not have barked because they would recognize him as a friend."

"Were the dogs familiar with his step and voice?"

"Yes. Only last Sunday he played with them for an hour, and later in the afternoon took them for a walk in the country."

"I see." Penfield stroked his chin reflectively. "When your sister told you of finding the burglar and his arrest, did you not, in the light of your wager, suspect that he might be Mr. Turnbull?"

"No." Barbara's eyes did not falter before his direct gaze. "I supposed that Mr. Turnbull meant to try and enter the house in his own proper person; it never dawned on me that he would resort to disguise. Besides," as the coroner started to make a remark, "we have had numerous robberies in our neighborhood, and the apartment house two blocks from us has had a regular epidemic of sneak thieves."

The coroner waited until Dr. Mayo, who had been writing with feverish haste, had picked up a fresh sheet of paper before resuming his examination.

"You accompanied your sister to the police court," he said. "Did you see the burglar there?"

"Yes."

"Did you realize his identity in the court room?"

"No. I only awoke to--to the situation when I saw him lying dead with his wig removed. The shock was frightful"--she closed her eyes for a second, for the room and the rows of faces confronting her were mixed in a maddening maze and she raised her hand to her swimming head. When she looked up she found Coroner Penfield by her side.

"That is all," he said kindly. "Please remain in the witness room, I may call you again," and he helped her down the step with careful attention.

Back in his corner Kent watched her departure. He was white to the lips.

"Heat too much for you?" asked a kindly-faced stranger, and Kent gave a mumbled "No," as he strove to pull himself together.

What deviltry was afoot? How dared the twins take such risks--to bear false witness was a grave criminal offense. He, alone, among all the spectators, had realized that in testifying before the inquest, the twins had swapped identities.

CHAPTER IX. "B-B-B"

The return of the morgue master to the platform caused Coroner Penfield to break off his whispered conversation with Dr. Mayo.

"Colonel McIntyre just telephoned that his car had a blow-out on the way here," explained the morgue master. "He will arrive shortly."

Penfield consulted a list of names. "Call Grimes, the McIntyre butler," he said. "We will hear him while waiting for the Colonel."

Grimes, small and thin, with the stolid countenance of the well-trained servant, was exceedingly short in his replies to the coroner's questions. Yes, he had lived with the McIntyre during their residence in Washington, something like five years, he couldn't quite remember the exact dates. No, there was never any quarreling, upstairs or down; it was a well-ordered household until this.

"Exactly," remarked the coroner dryly. "What about Monday night? Tell us, Grimes, what occurred in that house between midnight Monday and five o'clock Tuesday morning."

"Haven't much to tell," was the grumpy response. "I went upstairs about half-past eleven and got down the next morning at the usual hour, seven o'clock."

"And you heard no disturbing sounds in the night?"

"No; sir. We wouldn't be likely to; the servants' rooms are all at the top of the house and the staircase leading to them has a brick wall on either side, like stairs leading to an ordinary attic, and there's a door at the bottom which shuts off all sound from below." It was the longest sentence the butler had indulged in and he paused for breath.

"Who closes the house at night. Grimes?"

"I do, sir."

"Why did you leave the window in the reception room open?"

"I didn't, sir," was the prompt denial. "I had just locked it when Mrs. Brewster came in, along with Colonel McIntyre and Mr. Clymer, and they sat down to talk. When I left the room the window was locked fast, and so was every door and window in the place," he declared aggressively. "I'll take my dying oath to it, sir." Penfield looked at Grimes; that he was telling the truth was unmistakable.

"Who sits up to let in the young ladies when they go to balls?" he asked.

"Generally no one, sir, because Colonel McIntyre accompanies them or calls for them, and he has his latch-key. Lately," added Grimes as an after-thought, "Miss Helen has been using a duplicate latch-key."

"Has Miss Barbara McIntyre a latch-key, also?" asked Penfield.

"No, sir, I believe not," the butler looked dubious. "I recall that Colonel McIntyre gave Miss Helen her key at the luncheon table, and he said, then, to Miss Barbara that he couldn't trust her with one because she would be sure to lose it, she is that careless."

The coroner asked the next question with such abruptness that the butler started.

"When did you last see Mr. Turnbull at the house?"

"Sunday afternoon." Grimes' reply was spoken with more than his accustomed quickness of speech. "Mr. Turnbull called twice, after a long time in the drawing room, he went away taking the police dogs with him, and later called to bring them back."

"Where were these dogs on Monday night?"

"I last saw them in the library," replied Grimes shortly.

"And where did you find them the next morning?" prompted the coroner.

"In the cellar," laconically.

"And what were they doing in the cellar?"

"Hunting rats."

"And how did the dogs get in the cellar?" inquired the coroner patiently. Grimes was not volunteering information, even if he could not be accused of holding it back.

"Some one must have let them down the back stairs," the butler admitted. "I don't know who it was."

"Which servant got downstairs ahead of you on Tuesday morning?"

"No one, sir; the cook over-slept, and she and the maids came down in a bunch ten minutes later."

"And who told you of the attempted burglary and the burglar's arrest?" asked Penfield.

"Miss Barbara. She asked us to hurry breakfast for her and Miss Helen 'cause they had to go at once to the police court; she didn't give any particulars, or nothing," added Grimes in an injured tone. "'Twarn't 'til Thomas and I saw the afternoon papers that we knew what had been going on in our own house."

"That is all, Grimes," announced Penfield, and the butler left the platform with the same stolid air he wore when he arrived. He was followed in the witness chair by the other McIntyre servants in succession. Their testimony added nothing to what he had said but simply confirmed his statements.

Kent, who had grown restless during the servants' monotonous testimony, forgot the oppressive atmosphere of the room on seeing Mrs. Brewster enter under the escort of the morgue master. Spying a vacant seat several rows ahead of where he was sitting, Kent, with a muttered apology to the people over whom he crawled in his efforts to get out, hurried into it just as the vivacious widow had finished taking the oath to "tell the truth and nothing but the truth," and seated herself, with much rustling of silk skirts in the witness chair.

"State your full name, madam," directed Coroner Penfield, eyeing her dainty beauty with admiration.

"Margaret Perry Brewster," she answered. "Widow of Louis C. Brewster. Both I and my late husband were born and lived in Los Angeles, California."

"Are you visiting the Misses McIntyre?"

"Yes." Mrs. Brewster spoke in a chatty impersonal manner. "I have been with them since the first of the month."

"Did you attend the Grosvenor dance?" asked the coroner.

"No; the affair was only given for the debutantes of last fall and did not include married people," she explained. "It was a warm night and Colonel McIntyre asked Mr. Benjamin Clymer, who was dining with him, and me, to go for a motor ride, leaving Barbara at the Grosvenors' en route. We did so, returning to the house about eleven o'clock, and sat talking until about midnight in the reception room, then Colonel McIntyre drove Mr. Clymer home, and I went to my room."

"Were you awakened by any noises during the night?" inquired Penfield.

"No; I heard no noises." Mrs. Brewster's charming smile was infectious

"When did you first learn of the supposed burglary and the death of James Turnbull?"

"The McIntyre twins told me about the tragedy on their return from the police court," answered Mrs. Brewster, and settled herself a little more comfortably in the witness chair.

"When you were in the reception room, Mrs. Brewster"--Penfield paused and studied his notes a second--"did you observe if the window was open or closed?"

"It was not open when we entered," she responded. "But the air in the room was stuffy and at my request Mr. Clymer raised the window."

"Did he close it later?"

She considered the question. "I really do not recall," she admitted finally. Her eyes strayed toward the door through which she had entered, and Penfield answered her unspoken thought.

"Just one more question," he said hurriedly. "Did you see the dogs on Monday night?"

"Yes. I heard them scratching at the door leading to the basement as I went upstairs, and so I turned around and went down and opened the door and let them run down into the cellar."

Penfield snapped shut his notebook. "I am greatly obliged, Mrs. Brewster; we will not detain you longer."

The morgue master stepped forward and helped the pretty widow down from the platform.

"Colonel McIntyre is here now," he told the coroner.

"Ah, then bring him in," and Penfield, while awaiting the arrival of the new witness, straightened the papers on his desk.

McIntyre looked straight ahead of him as he walked down the room and stood frowning heavily while the oath was being administered, but his manner, when the coroner addressed him, had regained all the suavity and polish which had first captivated Washington society.

"I have been a resident of Washington for about five years," he said in answer to the coroner's question. "My daughters attended school here after their return from Paris, where they were in a convent for four years. They made their debut last November at our home in this city."

"Were you aware of the wager between your daughter Barbara and James Turnbull?" asked Penfield.

"I heard of it Sunday afternoon but paid little attention," admitted McIntyre. "My daughter Barbara's vagaries I seldom take seriously."

"Was Mr. Turnbull a frequent visitor at your house?"

"Oh, yes."

"Was he engaged to your daughter Helen?"

"No." McIntyre's denial was prompt and firmly spoken. Penfield and Kent, from his new seat nearer the platform, watched the colonel narrowly, but learned nothing from his expression.

"I have heard otherwise," observed the coroner dryly.

"You have been misinformed," McIntyre's manner was short. "I would suggest, Mr. Coroner, that you confine your questions and conjectures to matters pertinent to this inquiry."

Penfield flushed as one of the jurors snickered, but he did not repeat his previous question, asking instead, "Was there good feeling between you and Mr. Turnbull?"

"I never quarreled with him," replied McIntyre. "I really saw little of him as, whenever he called at the house, he came to see one or the other of my daughters, or both."

"When did you last see Mr. Turnbull?" inquired Penfield.

"He was at the house on Sunday and I had quite a talk with him." McIntyre leaned back in his chair and regarded the neat crease in his trousers with critical eyes. "I last saw Turnbull going out of the street door."

"Were you disturbed by the burglar's entrance on Monday night?"

McIntyre shook his head. "I am a heavy sleeper," he said. "I regret very much that my daughter Helen did not at once awaken me on finding the burglar, as she supposed, hiding in the closet. I knew nothing of the affair until Grimes informed me of it, and only reached the police court in time to bring my daughters home from the distressing scene following the identification of the dead burglar as Jimmie Turnbull."

"Colonel McIntyre," Penfield turned over several papers until he found the one he sought. "Mrs. Brewster has testified that while you and she were sitting in the reception room, Mr. Clymer opened the window. Did you close it on leaving the room?"

McIntyre reflected before answering. "I cannot remember doing so," he stated finally. "Clymer was in rather a hurry to leave, and after bidding Mrs. Brewster good night, we went straight out to the car and I drove him to the Saratoga."

"Then you cannot swear to the window having been re-locked?"

"I cannot."

Penfield paused a moment. "Did you return immediately to your house from the Saratoga apartment?"

"I did" promptly. "My chauffeur, Harris, wasn't well, and I wanted him to get home."

Penfield thought a moment before putting the next question.

"How did Miss Barbara return from the Grosvenor dance?" he asked.

"She was brought home by friends, Colonel and Mrs. Chase." McIntyre in turning about in his chair knocked down his walking stick from its resting place against its side, and the unexpected clatter made several women, nervously inclined, jump in their seats. Observing them, McIntyre smiled and was still smiling amusedly when Penfield addressed him.

"Did you observe many lights burning in your house when you returned?" asked Penfield.

"No, only those which are usually left lit at night."

"Was your daughter Helen awake?"

"I do not know. Her room was in darkness when I walked past her door on my way to bed."

Penfield removed his eye-glasses and polished them on his silk handkerchief. "I have no further questions to ask. Colonel, you are excused."

McIntyre bowed gravely to him and as he left the platform came face to face with his family physician, Dr. Stone.

Penfield, who was an old acquaintance of the physician's, signed to him to come on the platform. After the preliminaries had been gone through, he shifted his chair around, the better to face Stone.

"Did you accompany the Misses McIntyre to the police court on Tuesday morning?" he asked.

"I did," responded the physician, "at Miss Barbara's request. She said her sister was not very well and they disliked going alone to the police court."

"Did she state why she did not ask her father to go with them?"

"Only that he had not fully recovered from an attack of tonsillitis, which I knew to be a fact, and they did not want him to over-tax his strength."

There was a moment's pause as the coroner, his attention diverted by a whispered word or two from the morgue master, referred to his notes before resuming his examination.

"Did you know James Turnbull?" he asked a second later.

"Yes, slightly."

"Did you recognize him in his burglar's disguise?"

"I did not"

"Had you any suspicion that the burglar was other than he seemed?"

"No."

Penfield picked up a memorandum handed him by Dr. Mayo and referred to it. "I understand, doctor, that you were the first to go to the burglar's aid when he became ill," he said. "Is that true?"

"Yes," Stone spoke with more animation. "Happening to glance inside the cage where the prisoner sat, I saw he was struggling convulsively for breath. With Mr. Clymer's assistance I carried him into an ante-room off the court, but before I had crossed its threshold Turnbull expired in my arms."

"Was he conscious before he died?"

At the question Kent bent eagerly forward. What would be the reply?

"I am not prepared to answer that with certainty," replied Dr. Stone cautiously. "As I picked him up I heard him stammer faintly: 'B-b-b.'"

Kent started so violently that the man next to him turned and regarded him for a moment, then, more interested in what was transpiring on the platform, promptly forgot his agitated neighbor.

"Was Turnbull delirious, doctor?" asked the coroner.

Stone shook his head in denial. "No," he stated. "I take it that he started to say 'Barbara,' and his breath failed him; at any rate I only caught the stuttered 'B-b-b.'"

Penfield did not immediately continue his examination, but when he did so his manner was stern.

"Doctor, what in your opinion caused Mr. Turnbull's death?"

"Judging superficially--I made no thorough examination," Stone explained parenthetically, "I should say that Mr. Rochester was right when he stated that Turnbull died from an acute attack of angina pectoris."

"How did Mr. Rochester come to make that assertion and where?"

"Immediately after Turnbull's death," replied Stone. "Mr. Rochester, who shared his apartment, defended him in court. Mr. Rochester was aware that Turnbull suffered from the disease, and Mr. Clymer, who was present, also knew it."

"And what is your opinion, doctor?" questioned Penfield.

Stone hesitated. "There was a distinct odor of amyl nitrite noticeable when I went to Turnbull's aid, and I concluded then that he had some heart trouble and had inhaled the drug to ward off an attack. It bears out Mr. Rochester's theory of death from angina pectoris."

"I see. Thank you, doctor. Please wait with the other witnesses; we may call you again," and with a sigh the busy physician resigned himself to spending another hour in the room reserved for the witnesses.

The next to take the witness stand was Deputy Marshal Grant. His testimony was short and concise,--and his description of the scene in the police court preceding Turnbull's death was listened to with deep attention by every one.

"Did the prisoner show any symptoms of illness before his heart attack?" asked Penfield.

"Not exactly illness," replied Grant slowly. "I noticed he didn't move very quickly; sort of shambled, as if he was weak in his legs. I've seen 'drunk and disorderlies' act just that way, and paid no particular attention to him. He did ask for a drink of water just after he returned to the cage."

"Did you give it to him?"

"No, an attendant gave the glass to Mr. Rochester who handed it to Mr. Turnbull."

Penfield regarded Grant in silence for a minute. "That is all," he announced, and with a polite bow the deputy marshal withdrew.

Detective Ferguson recognized Kent as he passed up the room to the platform and gave him a slight bow and smile, but the smile had disappeared when, at the coroner's request, he told of his arrival just after the discovery of the burglar's identity.

"I searched the cage where the prisoner had been seated and found this handkerchief," he went on to say. "It had been dropped by Turnbull and was saturated with amyl nitrite. I had it examined by a chemist, who said that this amyl nitrite was given to patients with heart trouble in little pearl capsules to be crushed in handkerchiefs and the fumes inhaled.

"The chemist also told me that"--the detective spoke with impressive seriousness, "judging from the number of particles of capsules adhering to the linen, more than one capsule had been crushed by Turnbull. Here is the handkerchief," and he laid it on the table with great care.

Kent's heart sank; the moment he had dreaded all that long afternoon had come. Penfield inspected the handkerchief with interest, and then passed it to the jurors, cautioning them to handle it carefully.

"I note," he stated, turning again to Detective Ferguson, "that it is a woman's handkerchief."

"It is," replied Ferguson. "And embroidered in one corner is the initial 'B.'"

Penfield ran his fingers through his gray hair. "You may go, Ferguson," he said, and beckoned to the morgue master. "Ask Miss Barbara McIntyre to return."

The girl was quick in answering the summons. Kent, more and more worried, was watching the scene with painful attention.

"Did Mr. Turnbull have one of your handkerchiefs?" asked Penfield.

Her surprise at the question was manifest in her manner.

"He might have," she said. "I have a dreadful habit of dropping my handkerchiefs around."

"Did you miss one after his visit to your house on Monday night?"

"Miss McIntyre," Penfield took up the handkerchief which the foreman replaced on his desk a moment before, and holding it with care extended it toward the girl. "Is this your handkerchief?"

She inspected the handkerchief and the initial with curiosity, but with nothing more, Kent was convinced, and in his relief was almost guilty of disturbing the decorum of the inquest with a shout of joy.

"It is not my handkerchief," she stated clearly.

Penfield replaced the handkerchief on the table with the same care he had picked it up, and turned again to her.

"Thank you, Miss McIntyre; I won't detain you longer. Logan," to the morgue master, "ask Dr. Stone to step here."

Almost immediately Stone reentered the room and hurried to the platform.

"Would two or more capsules of amyl nitrite constitute a lethal dose?" asked Penfield.

"They would be very apt to finish a feeble heart," replied Stone. "Three capsules, if inhaled deeply would certainly kill a healthy person."

Penfield showed the handkerchief to the physician. "Can a chemist tell, from the particles clinging to this handkerchief, how many capsules have been used?"

"I should say he could." Stone looked grave as he inspected the linen, taking careful note of the letter "B" in one corner of the handkerchief. "But there is this to be considered--Turnbull may not have crushed those capsules all at the same time."

"What do you mean?"

"He may have felt an attack coming on earlier in the evening and used a capsule, and in the police court used the same handkerchief in the same manner."

"I see," Penfield nodded. "The point is cleverly taken."

Kent silently agreed with the coroner. The next instant Stone was excused, and after a slight pause the deputy coroner, Dr. Mayo, left his table and his notes and occupied the witness chair, after first being sworn. The preliminaries did not consume much time, and Penfield's manner was brisk as he addressed his assistant.

"Did you make a post-mortem examination of Turnbull?" he asked.

"I did, sir, in the presence of the morgue master and Dr. McLane." Dr. Mayo displayed an anatomical chart, drawing his pencil down it as he talked. "We found from the condition of the heart that the deceased had suffered from angina pectoris"--he paused and spoke more slowly--"in examining the gastric contents we found the presence of aconitine."

"Aconitine?" questioned Penfield, and the reporters, scenting the sensational, leaned forward eagerly so as not to miss the deputy coroner's answer.

"Aconitine, an active poison," he explained. "It is the alkaloid of aconite, and generally fatal in its results."

CHAPTER X. AT THE CLUB DE VINGT

The large building of the popular Club de Vingt, or as one Washingtonian put it, the "Club De Vin," which had sprung into existence in the National Capital during the war, was ablaze with light and Benjamin Clymer, sitting at a small table in one corner of the dining-room, wished most heartily that it had been less crowded.

Many dinner-parties were being given that night, and it was only by dint of perseverance and a Treasury note that he had finally induced the head waiter to put in an extra table for him and his guest, Harry Kent. Kent had been very late and, to add to his short-comings, had been silent, not to say morose, during dinner. Clymer heaved a sigh of relief when the table was cleared and coffee and cigars placed before them.

Kent roused himself from his abstraction. "We cannot talk here," he said, looking at the gay diners who surrounded them. "And I have several important matters to discuss with you, Mr. Clymer."

His remark was overheard by their waiter, and he stopped pouring out Kent's coffee.

"There is a small smoking room to the right of the dining room," he suggested. "I passed there but a moment ago and it was not occupied. If you desire, sir, I will serve coffee there."

"An excellent idea." Clymer rose quickly and he and Kent followed the waiter to the inclosed porch which had been converted into an attractive lounging room for the club members. It was much cooler than the over-heated dining room, and Kent was grateful for the subdued light given out by the artistically shaded lamps with which it was furnished. There was silence while the waiter with deft fingers arranged the coffee and cigars on a wicker table; then receiving Clymer's generous tip with a word of thanks, the man departed.

Kent wheeled his chair around so as to face his companion and still have a side view of the dining room, where tables were being rapidly removed for the dance which followed dinners on Thursday nights. Clymer selected a cigar with care and, leaning back in his chair until the wicker creaked under his weight, he waited patiently for Kent to speak. It was fully five minutes before Kent addressed him.

"So James Turnbull was poisoned after all," he commented. "A week ago I would have sworn that Jimmie hadn't an enemy in the world."

"Ah, but he had; and a very bitter vindictive enemy, if the evidence given at the coroner's inquest this afternoon is to be believed," replied Clymer seriously. "The case is remarkably puzzling."

"It is." Kent bit savagely at his cigar as a slight vent to his feelings. "'Killed by a dose of aconitine by a person or persons unknown,' was the jury's verdict, and a nice tangle they have left me to ferret out."

"You?"

"Yes. I'm going to solve this mystery if it is a possible thing." Kent's tone was grim. "And Colonel McIntyre only gave me until Saturday night to work in."

Clymer eyed him in surprise. "McIntyre desires to get back his lost securities; judging from his comments after the inquest, he is not particularly interested in who killed Turnbull."

"But I am," exclaimed Kent. "The more I think of it, the more convinced I am that the forged letter, with the subsequent disappearance of McIntyre's securities has some connection with Jimmie's untimely death, be it murder or suicide."

"Suicide?" Clymer's raised eyebrows indicated his surprise.

"Yes," shortly. "Aconitine would have killed just as surely if swallowed with suicidal intent as if administered with murderous design."

A pause followed which neither man seemed anxious to break, then Kent turned to the banker, and the latter noticed the haggard lines in his face.

"Listen to me, Mr. Clymer," he began. "My instinct tells me that Jimmie Turnbull never forged that letter or stole McIntyre's securities, but I admit that everything points to his guilt, even his death."

"How so?"

"Because the theft of the securities supplies a motive for his suicide--fear of exposure and imprisonment," argued Kent. "But there is no motive, so far as I can see, for Jimmie's murder. Men don't kill each other without a motive."

"There is homicidal mania," suggested Clymer.

"But not in this case," retorted Kent. "We are sane men and it is up to us to find out if Jimmie died by his own hand or was killed by some unknown enemy."

"Rest easy, Mr. Kent," said a voice from the doorway and Kent, who had turned his back in that direction the better to talk to Clymer, whirled around and found Detective Ferguson regarding him just inside the threshold. "Mr. Turnbull's enemy is not unknown and will soon be under arrest."

"Who is he?" demanded Clymer and Kent simultaneously.

"Philip Rochester."

Clymer was the first to recover from his astonishment. "Oh, get out!" he exclaimed incredulously. "Why, Rochester was Turnbull's most intimate friend."

"Until they fell in love with the same girl," answered Ferguson succinctly, taking possession of the only other chair the porch boasted. "One quarrel led to another and then Rochester did for him. Oh, it dove-tails nicely; motive, jealous anger; opportunity, recognition in court of Turnbull disguised as a burglar, at the same time Rochester learns that Turnbull has been caught after midnight in the house of his sweetheart--"

"D--mn you!" Kent sprang for the detective's throat. "Cut out your abominable insinuations. Miss McIntyre shall not be insulted."

"I'm not insulting her," gasped Ferguson, half strangled. "Let go, Mr. Kent. I'm only telling you what that half crazy partner of yours, Rochester, was probably thinking in the police court. Let go, I say."

Clymer aided the detective in freeing himself. "Sit down, Kent," he said sternly. "Ferguson meant no offense. Go ahead, man, and tell us the rest of your theories."

It was some minutes, however, before the detective had collected sufficient breath to answer intelligently.

"I size it up this way," he began with a resentful glance at Kent who had dropped back in his chair again. "Rochester knew his friend had heart disease and that his sudden death would be attributed to it--so he took a sporting chance and administered a fatal dose of aconitine."

"How was it done?" asked Clymer.

"Just slipped the poison into the glass of water he handed to Turnbull in the court room," explained Ferguson, and glanced in triumph at Kent. "Neat, wasn't it?"

Kent regarded the detective, his mind in a whirl. His theory was certainly plausible, but--"Have you other evidence to prove, your theory?" he asked.

"Yes." Ferguson checked off his points on his fingers. "Remember how insistent Mr. Rochester was that Turnbull had died from angina pectoris?"

"I do," acknowledged Clymer, deeply interested. "Continue, Ferguson."

The detective needed no second bidding.

"Another point," he began. "There never would have been a post-mortem examination if Miss Helen McIntyre hadn't asked for it. She knew of the ill-feeling between the men and suspected foul play on Rochester's part."

"Wait," commanded Kent. "Has Miss McIntyre substantiated that statement?"

"Not yet," admitted Ferguson. "I stopped at her house, but the butler said the young ladies had retired and could not see any one." Kent, who had called there on the way to keep his dinner engagement with Clymer, had been met with the same statement, to his bitter disappointment. He most earnestly desired to see the twins and to see them together, to make one more effort to induce them to confide in him; for that they had some secret trouble he was convinced; he longed to be of aid, but his hands were tied through lack of information.

"Don't imply motives to Miss McIntyre's act until you have verified them, Ferguson," he cautioned. "Go on with your theories."

"One moment," Clymer broke into the conversation. "Did Rochester tell you, Ferguson, that he had recognized Turnbull in his burglar disguise?"

"No, sir; I never had an opportunity to ask him, for he disappeared Tuesday night and has not been seen or heard of since," Ferguson rejoined.

"Hold on," Kent checked him with an impatient gesture. "I had a telegram from Rochester this morning, stating he was in Cleveland."

"I didn't forget about the telegram," retorted Ferguson. "It was to consult you about that, that I hunted you up to-night. That telegram was bogus."

"What!" Kent half rose from his chair.

"Yes. After the inquest I called Cleveland on the long distance, talked with the City Club officials and with Police Headquarters; all declared that Rochester was not there, and no trace could be found of his having ever arrived in the city."

Clymer laid down his half smoked cigar and stared at the detective.

"You think then that Rochester has bolted?" he asked.

"It looks that way," insisted Ferguson. "How about it, Mr. Kent?" The question was put with a touch of arrogance.

Kent did not reply immediately. Every fact that Ferguson had brought out fitted the situation, and Rochester's disappearance added color to the detective's charges. Why was he hiding unless from guilty motives, and where had he gone? Kent shook a bewildered head.

"It is plausible," he conceded, "but, after all, only circumstantial evidence."

"Well, circumstantial evidence is good enough for me to work on," retorted Ferguson. "On discovering that the telegram from Cleveland was a hoax, I concluded Ferguson might be lurking around Washington and so sent a description of him to the different precincts and secured a search warrant."

"You did?"

"Yes. Armed with it I visited Mr. Rochester's apartment, but couldn't find a clew to his present whereabouts," admitted Ferguson. "So then I went to your office, Mr. Kent, and ransacked the firm's safe."

"Confound you!" Kent leaned forward in his wrath and shook his fist at the detective. "What right had you to do such a thing?"

"The search warrant covered it," explained Ferguson. "I could look through your safe, Mr. Kent, because Rochester was your senior partner and you shared the office together; I was within the law."

"Perhaps you were," Kent controlled his anger with an effort. "But I had told you I did not know Rochester's whereabouts before I showed you the Cleveland telegram, which you claim is bogus."

"It's bogus, all right," insisted the detective. "I thought it just possible I might find some paper which would give me a clew to Rochester's hiding place, so I went through the safe."

"How did you get it open?" asked Kent.

"I found it open."

Kent leapt to his feet. "You--found--it open!"--he stammered. "Why, man, I locked that safe securely just before I left the office at six o'clock."

"Sure?"

"Absolutely certain."

"Were you alone?"

"Yes, all alone. Sylvester left at five o'clock"

"Who knew the combination of the safe?"

"Only Rochester and I."

It was Ferguson's turn to spring up "By--!" he exclaimed. "I thought the electric bulbs in the office felt warm, as if they had recently been burning--Rochester must have been there just before me."

"It would seem that Rochester is still in the city," remarked Clymer. "Do you know, Kent, whether he had his office keys with him?"

"I presume so," Kent slipped his hand inside his pocket and took out a bunch of keys. "He left these duplicates in his desk at the office."

"Sure they are duplicates?" questioned Ferguson, and Kent flushed.

"I know they are," he retorted. "Rochester had them made over a year ago as a matter of convenience, for he was always forgetting his keys, and kept these at our office."

"He's a queer cuss," was the detective's only comment and Clymer broke into the conversation.

"Did you find any address or paper in the safe which might prove a clew, Ferguson?" he inquired.

"Nothing, not even a scrap of paper," and the detective's tone was glum.

"Did the safe look as if its contents had been tumbled about?" asked Kent.

"No, everything seemed in order." Ferguson thrust his hand inside his coat pocket. "There was one envelope in the right hand compartment which puzzled me--"

"Hold on--was that compartment also unlocked?" asked Kent.

"It was," not giving Kent time to speak again Ferguson continued his remarks. "As this was unaddressed I brought it to you, Mr. Kent, to ask if it was your personal property"--he drew out the white envelope which Helen McIntyre had brought Kent that morning and turned it over so that both men could see the large red seal bearing the letter "B."

"It is my property," asserted Kent instantly.

"Would you mind opening it?" asked Ferguson.

"I would, most certainly; it relates to my personal affairs."

Ferguson looked a trifle non-plussed. "Would you mind telling me its contents, Mr. Kent?" he asked persuasively.

Kent regarded the detective squarely. He could not betray Helen, the envelope might contain harmless nonsense, but she had placed it in his safe-keeping--no, confound it, she had left it in the safe for Rochester--and Rochester was apparently a fugitive from justice, while circumstantial evidence pointed to his having poisoned Helen's lover, Jimmie...

"If you must know, Ferguson," Kent spoke with deliberation. "They are old love letters of mine."

Clymer glanced down at the envelope which the detective still held, the red seal making a distinct blotch of color on the white, glazed surface.

"Ah, Kent," he said in amusement. "So rumor is right in predicting your engagement to Barbara McIntyre. Good luck to you!"

Through the open doorway to the dining room where the dancing had ceased for the moment, came a soft laugh and Mrs. Brewster looked in at them. McIntyre, standing like her shadow, gazed in curiosity over her shoulder at the three men.

"How jolly to find you," cooed Mrs. Brewster. "And what a charming retreat! It's much too nice to be occupied by men, only." She inclined her head in a little gracious bow to Ferguson and stepped inside.

"Have my chair," suggested Clymer hospitably as the pretty widow raised her lorgnette and scanned the Oriental hangings and lamps, and lastly, the white envelope which lay on the table, red seal uppermost, where Ferguson had placed it on her entrance.

"Are your daughters here, Colonel McIntyre?" asked Kent as he took a step toward the table. McIntyre's answer was drowned in an outburst of cheering in the dining room and the rush of many feet. On common impulse Kent and the others turned toward the doorway and looked inside the dining room. Two officers of the French High Commission were being held on the shoulders of comrades and were delivering, as best they could amidst cheers and applause, their farewell to hospitable Washington.

As his companions brushed by him to join the gay throng in the center of the room, Kent turned back to pick up the envelope he had left lying on the table. It was gone.

In feverish haste Kent looked under the table, under the chairs, the lounge and its cushions, behind the draperies, and even under the rugs which covered the floor of the porch, and then rose and stared into the dining room. Which one of his companions had taken the envelope?

Outside the porch the beautiful trumpet vine, its sturdy trunk and thick branches reaching almost to the roof of the club building, rustled as in a high wind, and the branches swayed this way and that as a figure climbed swiftly down from the porch until, reaching the fence separating the club property from its neighbor's, the man swung across it, no mean athletic feet, and taking advantage of each sheltering shadow, darted into the alley and from there down silent, deserted Nineteenth Street.

CHAPTER XI. HALF A TRUTH

Dancing was being resumed in the dining room as Kent appeared again in the doorway and he made his way as quickly as possible among the couples, going into all the rooms on that floor, but nowhere could he find Detective Ferguson. On emerging from the drawing room, he encountered the steward returning from downstairs.

"Have you seen Mr. Clymer?" he asked hurriedly.

"Yes, Mr. Kent; he just left the club, taking Detective Ferguson with him in his motor. Is there anything I can do?" added the steward observing Kent's agitation.

"No, no, thanks. Say, where is Colonel McIntyre?" Kent gave up further pursuit of the detective, he could find him later at Headquarters. The steward looked among the dancers. "I don't see him," he said, "But there is Mrs. Brewster dancing in the front room; the Colonel must be somewhere around. If I meet him, Mr. Kent, shall I tell him you are looking for him?"

"I will be greatly obliged if you will do so," replied Kent, and straightening his tie, he went in quest of the pretty widow. He had found her a merry chatter-box in the past, possibly he could gain valuable information from her. He found Mrs. Brewster just completing her dance with a fine looking Italian officer whose broad breast bore many military decorations.

"Dance the encore with me"--Kent could be very persuasive when he wished, and Mrs. Brewster dimpled with pleasure, but there was a faint indecision in her manner which he was quick to note. What prompted it? He had been on friendly terms with her; in fact, she had openly championed his cause, so Barbara had once told him, when Colonel McIntyre had made caustic remarks about his frequent calls at the McIntyre house.

"Just one turn," she said, as the foreigner bowed and withdrew. "I am feeling a little weary to-night--the strain of the inquest," she, added in explanation.

"Perhaps you would rather sit out the dance," he suggested. "There is an alcove in that window; oh, pshaw!" as a man and a girl took possession of the chairs.

"Never mind, we can roost on the stairs," Mrs. Brewster preceded him to the staircase leading to the third floor, and sat down, bracing her back very comfortably against the railing, while Kent seated himself at her feet on the lower step. "Extraordinary developments at the inquest this afternoon," he began, as she volunteered no remark. "To think of Jimmie Turnbull being poisoned!"

"It is unbelievable," she said, and her vehemence was a surprise to Kent; he knew her as all froth and bubble. What had brought the dark circles under her eyes and the unwonted seriousness in her manner?

"Unbelievable, yes," he agreed gravely. "But true; the autopsy ended all doubt."

"You mean it developed doubt," she corrected, and a sigh accompanied the words. "Have the police any clew to the guilty man?"

"I don't know, I'm sure," Kent spoke with caution.

"You don't?" Her voice was a little sharp. "Didn't Detective Ferguson give you any news when talking to you on the porch?"

"So you recognized the detective?"

"I? No; I have never seen him before"--she nodded gayly to an acquaintance passing through the hall. "Colonel McIntyre told me his name. It was so odd to meet a man here not in evening clothes that I had to ask who he was."

"Ferguson came to bring me some papers about a personal matter," explained Kent. He turned so as to face her. "Did you see a white envelope lying on the table when you walked out on the porch?"

She bowed her head absently, her foot keeping time to the inspiring music played by the orchestra stationed on the stair landing just above where they sat. "You left it lying on the table."

"Yes, so I did," replied Kent. "And I believe I was so ungallant as to bolt into the dining room in front of you. Please accept my apologies." Behind her fan, which she used with languid grace, the widow watched him.

"We all bolted together," she responded, "and are equally guilty--"

"Of what?" questioned a voice from the background, and looking up Kent saw Colonel McIntyre standing on the step above Mrs. Brewster. The music had ceased and in the lull their conversation had been distinctly audible.

"Guilty of curiosity," finished the widow.

"Colonel de Geofroy's farewell speech was very amusing, did you not think so?"

"I did not stay to hear it," Kent confessed. "I had to return to the porch and get my envelope."

"You were a long time about it," commented McIntyre, sitting down by Mrs. Brewster and possessing himself of her fan. "I waited to tell you that Helen and Barbara were worn out after the inquest and so stayed at home to-night, but you didn't show up."

"Neither did the envelope," retorted Kent, and as his companions looked at him, he added. "It had disappeared off the table."

"Probably blew away," suggested McIntyre. "I noticed a strong current of air from the dining room, and two of the windows inclosing the porch were open."

"That's hardly possible," Kent replied skeptically. "The envelope weighed at least two ounces; it would have taken quite a gale to budge it."

McIntyre turned red. "Are you insinuating that one of us walked off with your envelope, Kent?" he demanded angrily. Mrs. Brewster stayed him as he was about to rise.

"Did you not say that Detective Ferguson brought you the envelope, Mr. Kent?" she asked.

"Yes."

"Then what more likely than that he carried it off again?" She smiled amusedly as Kent's expression altered. "Why not ask the detective?"

Her suggestion held a grain of truth. Suppose Ferguson had not believed his statement that the papers in the envelope were his personal property and had taken the envelope away to examine it at his leisure? The thought brought Kent to his feet.

"Good night, Mrs. Sherlock Holmes," he said jestingly, "I'll follow your advice"--There was no opportunity to say more, for several men had discovered the widow's perch on the stairs and came to claim their dances. Over their heads McIntyre watched Kent stride downstairs, then stooping over he picked up Mrs. Brewster's fan and sat down to patiently await her return.

Kent's pursuit of the detective took longer than he had anticipated, and it was after midnight before he finally located him at the office of the Chief of Detectives in the District Building. "I've called for the envelope you took from my safe early this evening," he began without preface, hardly waiting for the latter's surprised greeting.

"Why, Mr. Kent, I left it lying on the porch table at the club," declared Ferguson. "Didn't you take it?"

"No." Kent's worried expression returned. "Like a fool I forgot the envelope when that cheering broke out in the dining room and rushed to find out what it was about; when I returned to the porch the envelope was gone.

"Disappeared?" questioned Ferguson in astonishment.

"Disappeared absolutely; I searched the porch thoroughly and couldn't find a trace of it," Kent explained. "And in spite of McIntyre's contention that it might have blown out of the window, I am certain it did not."

"The windows were open, and I recollect there was a strong draught," remarked Ferguson thoughtfully. "But not sufficient to carry away that envelope."

"Exactly." Kent stepped closer. "Did you observe which one of our companions stood nearest the porch table?"

Ferguson eyed him curiously. "Say, are you insinuating that one of those people took your envelope?"

"Yes."

A subdued whistle escaped Ferguson. "What was in that envelope. Mr. Kent," he demanded, "to make it of any value to that bunch?" and as Kent did not answer immediately, he added, "Are you sure it had nothing to do with Jimmie Turnbull's death and Philip Rochester's disappearance?"

"Quite sure." Kent's gaze did not waver before his penetrating look. "I have already told you that the envelope contained old love letters, and I very naturally do not wish them to fall into the hands of Colonel McIntyre, the father of the girl I hope to marry."

Ferguson smiled understandingly. "I see. From what I know of Colonel McIntyre there's a very narrow, nagging spirit concealed under his frank and engaging manner; I wish you joy of your future father-in-law," and he chuckled.

"Thanks," dryly. "You haven't answered my question as to who stood nearest the porch table, Ferguson."

The detective looked thoughtful. "We all stood fairly near; perhaps Mrs. Brewster was a shade the nearest. Mr. Clymer was offering her a chair when that noise came from the dining room. There's one thing I am willing to swear to"--his manner grew more earnest--"that envelope was still lying on the table when I hustled into the dining room."

"Well, who was the last person to leave the porch?" Kent demanded eagerly.

"I don't know," was the disappointing answer. "I reached the door at the same moment you did and passed right around the dining room to get a view of what was going on. I thought I would take a squint at the tables and see if there was any wine being used," he admitted. "But there was nothing doing in that line. Then Mr. Clymer offered to bring me down to Headquarters, and I left the club with him."

Kent took a turn about the room. "Did Mr. Clymer go to the Cosmos Club?" he asked, pausing by the detective.

"No, I heard him tell his chauffeur to drive to the Saratoga. Want to use the telephone?" observing Kent's glance stray to the instrument.

By way of answer Kent took off the receiver and after giving a number to Central, he recognized Clymer's voice over the telephone.

"That you, Mr. Clymer? Yes, well, this is Kent speaking. Can you tell me who was the last person to leave the porch when Colonel de Geofroy made his farewell speech to-night at the club?"

"I was," came Clymer's surprised answer.

"I waited for McIntyre to pick up Mrs. Brewster's fan."

"Did he take my letter off the table also?" called Kent.

"Why, no." Clymer's voice testified to his increased surprise. "Mrs. Brewster dropped her fan right in the doorway just as McIntyre and I approached; we both stooped to get it and, like fools; bumped our heads together in the act. He got the fan, however, and I waited for him to walk into the dining room before following Mrs. Brewster."

"As you passed the table, Mr. Clymer, did you see my letter lying on the table?" persisted Kent.

"Upon my word I never looked at the table," Clymer's hearty tone carried conviction. "I walked right along in my hurry to know what the cheering was about. I am sorry, Kent; have you mislaid your letter?"

"Yes," glumly. "Sorry to have disturbed you, Mr. Clymer; good night," and Clymer's echoing, "Good night" sounded faintly as he hung up the receiver.

"Drew blank," he announced, turning to Ferguson. "Confound you, Ferguson; you had no right to touch the papers in my safe. If harm comes from it, I'll make you suffer," and not waiting for the detective's jumbled apologies and explanations, he hurried from the building. But once on the sidewalk he paused for thought. McIntyre must have picked up the white envelope, there was no other feasible explanation of its disappearance. But what had attracted his attention to the envelope--the red seal with the big letter "B" was its only identifying mark. If Helen had only told him the contents of the envelope!

Kent struck his clenched fist in his left hand in wrath; something must be done, he could not stand there all night. Although it was through no fault of his own that he had lost the envelope entrusted to his care, he was still responsible to Helen for its disappearance. She must be told that it was gone, however unpleasant the task.

Kent walked hastily along Pennsylvania Avenue until he came to a drug store still open, and entered the telephone booth. He had recollected that the twins had a branch telephone in their sitting room; he would have to chance their being awake at that hour.

Barbara McIntyre turned on her pillow and rubbed her sleepy eyes; surely she had been mistaken in thinking she heard the telephone bell ringing. Even as she lay striving to listen, she dozed off again, to be rudely awakened by Helen's voice at her ear.

"Babs!" came the agitated whisper. "The envelope's gone."

"Gone!" Barbara swung out of bed.

"Gone where?"

"Father has it."

Downstairs in the library Mrs. Brewster paused on her entrance by the side of a piece of carved Venetian furniture and laying her coronation scarf on it, she examined a white envelope--the red seal was intact.

At the sound of approaching footsteps she raised a trap door in the piece of furniture and only her keen ears caught the faint thud of the envelope as it dropped inside, then with a happy, tender smile she turned to meet Colonel McIntyre.

CHAPTER XII. THE ECHO OF A LAUGH

Colonel McIntyre tramped the deserted dining room in exasperation. Nine o'clock and the twins had not come to breakfast, nor was there any evidence that Mrs. Brewster intended taking that meal downstairs.

"Will you wait any longer, sir?" inquired Grimes, who hovered solicitously in the background. "I'm afraid, sir, your eggs will be over-done."

"Bring them along," directed McIntyre, and flung himself into his chair at the foot of the table. He had been seated but a few minutes when Barbara appeared and dutifully presented her cheek to be kissed, then she tripped lightly to Helen's place opposite her father, and pressed the electric bell for Grimes.

"Coffee, please," she said as that worthy appeared, and busied herself in arranging the cups and saucers. "Helen is taking her breakfast upstairs," she explained to her father.

"How about Mrs. Brewster?"

"Still asleep." Barbara poured out her father's coffee with careful attention to detail. "I peeked into her room a moment ago and she looked so 'comfy' I hadn't the heart to awaken her. You must have been very late at the club last night."

"We got home a little after one o'clock."

McIntyre helped himself to poached eggs and bacon. "What did you do last night?"

"Went to bed early," answered Barbara with brevity. "Helen wasn't feeling well."

McIntyre's handsome face showed concern as he glanced across the table. "Have you sent for Dr. Stone?"

"No."

"Why not?"

"Helen--I--we"--Barbara stumbled in her speech. "We have taken an aversion to Dr. Stone."

McIntyre set down his coffee cup with unwonted force, thereby spilling some of its contents.

"What!" he exclaimed in complete astonishment, and regarded her fixedly for a moment. His tolerant manner, which he frequently assumed toward Barbara, grew stern. "Dr. Stone is my personal friend, as well as our family physician--"

"And a cousin of Margaret Brewster," put in Barbara mildly.

"Well, what of it?" trenchantly, aware that he had colored at mention of the widow's name. "Nothing," Barbara's eyes opened innocently. "I only recalled the fact of his relationship as you enumerated his virtues."

Colonel McIntyre transferred his regard from her to the butler. "You need not wait, Grimes." He remained silent until the servant was safely in the pantry, and then addressed his daughter. "None of your tricks, Barbara," he cautioned. "If Helen is ill enough to require medical attention, Dr. Stone is to be sent for, regardless of your sudden dislike to him, for which, by the way, you have given no cause."

"Haven't I?" Barbara folded her napkin with neat exactness. "It's--it's intangible."

"Pooh!" McIntyre gave a short laugh, as he pushed back his chair. "I'm going to see Helen. And Barbara," stopping on his way to the door, "don't be a fool."

Barbara rubbed the tiny mole under the lobe of her ear, a trick she had when absent-minded or in deep thought. "Helen," she announced, unaware that she spoke loud, "shall have a physician, but it won't be--why, Grimes," awakening to the servant's noiseless return. "You can take the breakfast dishes. Did Miss Helen eat anything?"

"Not very much, miss." Grimes shook a troubled head. "But she done better than at dinner last night, so she's picking up, and don't you be worried over her," with emphasis, as he sidled nearer. "Tell me, miss, is the colonel courtin' Mrs. Brewster?"

"Ask him," she suggested and smiled at the consternation which spread over the butler's face.

"Me, miss!" he exclaimed in horror. "It would be as much as my place is worth; the colonel's that quick-tempered. Why, miss, just because I tidied up his desk and put his papers to rights he flew into a terrible passion."

"When was that?"

"Early this morning, miss; and he so upset Thomas, miss, that he gave notice."

"Oh, that's too bad." Barbara liked the second man. "Perhaps father will reconsider and persuade him to stay."

The butler looked unconvinced. "It was about the police dogs," he confided to her. "Thomas told him that Miss Helen wanted them brought back, and the colonel swore at him--'twas more than Thomas could stand and he ups and goes." Barbara halted half way to the door. "Did Thomas get the dogs?"

"You wait and see, miss." Grimes was guilty of a most undignified wink. "Thomas ain't forgiven himself for not being here Monday night, miss; though it wouldn't a done him any good; he wouldn't a heard Mr. Turnbull climbing in or his arrest, away upstairs in the servants' quarters."

"Grimes," Barbara retracted her footsteps and placed her lips very close to the old servant's ear.

"When I came in on Tuesday morning I found the door to the attic stairway standing partly open...

"Did you now, miss?" The two regarded each other warily. "And what hour may that have been?"

The butler cocked his ear for her answer--'he was sometimes a little hard of hearing; but he waited in vain, Barbara had disappeared inside the library.

Colonel McIntyre had not gone at once to see his daughter Helen, as Barbara had supposed from his remark, instead he went down the staircase and into the reception room on the ground floor. It was generally used as a smoking room and lounge, but when entertaining was done, cloaks and wraps were left there. McIntyre looked over the prettily upholstered furniture, then strolled to the window and carefully inspected the lock; it appeared in perfect order as he tested it. Pushing the catch back as far as it would go, he raised the window--the sash moved upward without a sound, and he leaned out and looked up and down the path which ran the depth of the house to the kitchen door and servants' entrance. There was an iron gate separating the path from the sidewalk, always kept locked at night, and McIntyre had thought that sufficient protection and had not put an iron grille in the window.

McIntyre closed and locked the window, then pulling out the gilt chair which stood in front of the desk, he sat down, selected some monogrammed paper and penned a few lines in his characteristic though legible writing. Picking up some red sealing wax, he lighted the small candle in its brass holder which matched the rest of the desk ornaments, but before heating the wax he looked for his signet ring, and frowned when he recalled leaving it on his dresser. He hesitated a moment, then catching sight of a silver seal lying at the back of the desk he picked it up and moistened the initial. A few minutes later he blew out the candle, returned the wax and seal to a pigeon hole, and carefully placed the envelope with its well stamped letter "B" in his coat pocket, and tramped upstairs.

Helen heard his heavy tread coming down the hall toward her room, and scrambled back to bed. She had but time to arrange her dressing sacque when her father walked in.

"Good morning, my dear," he said and, stooping over, kissed her. As he straightened up, the side of his single-breasted coat turned back and exposed to Helen's bright eyes the end of a white envelope. "Barbara told me you are not well," he wheeled forward a chair and sat down by the bed. "Hadn't I better send for Dr. Stone?" "Oh, no," her reply, though somewhat faint, was emphatic, and he frowned.

"Why not?" aggressively. "I trust you do not share Barbara's suddenly developed prejudice against the good doctor."

"I do not require a physician," she said evasively. "I am well."

McIntyre regarded her vexedly. He could not decide whether her flushed cheeks were from fever or the result of exertion or excitement. Excitement over what? He looked about the room; it reflected the taste of its dainty owner in its furnishings, but nowhere did he find an answer to his unspoken question, until his eye lighted on a box of rouge under the electric lamp on her bed stand.

"Don't use that," he said, touching the box.

"You know I detest make-up."

"Oh, that!" She turned to see what he was talking about. "That rouge belongs to Margaret Brewster."

McIntyre promptly changed the conversation. "Have you had your breakfast?" he asked.

"Yes; Grimes took the tray down some time ago." Helen watched her father fidget with his watch fob for several minutes, then asked with characteristic directness. "What do you wish?"

"To see that you have proper medical attention if you are ill," he returned promptly. "How would a week or ten days at Atlantic City suit you and Barbara?"

"Not at all." Helen sat up from her reclining position on the pillows. "You forget, father, that we have a house-guest; Margaret Brewster is not leaving until May."

"I had not forgotten," curtly. "I propose that she go with us."

A faint "Oh!" escaped Helen, otherwise she made no comment, and McIntyre, after contemplating her for a minute, looked away.

"Either go to Atlantic City with us, Helen, or resume your normal, everyday life," he said shortly. "I am tired of heroics; Jimmie Turnbull was hardly the man to inspire them."

"Stop!" Helen's voice rang out imperiously. "I will not permit one word said in disparagement of Jimmie, least of all from you, father. Wait," as he attempted to speak. "I do not know what traits of character I may have inherited from you, but I have all mother's loyalty, and--that loyalty belongs to Jimmie."

McIntyre's eyes shifted under her gaze.

"I regret very much this obsession," he said rising. "I will not attempt to reason with you again, Helen, but"--he made no effort to lower his voice, "the world--our world will soon know what manner of man James Turnbull was, of that I am determined."

"And I"--Helen faced her father proudly--"I will leave no stone unturned to defend his memory."

Her father wheeled about. "In doing so, see that you do not compromise yourself," he remarked coldly, and before the infuriated girl could answer, he slammed the door shut and stalked downstairs.

Some half hour later he opened the door of Rochester and Kent's law office and would have walked unceremoniously into Kent's private office had not John Sylvester stepped forward from behind his desk in the corner.

"Good morning, Colonel," he said civilly. "Mr. Kent is not here. Do you wish to leave any message?"

"Oh, good morning, Sylvester," McIntyre's manner was brusque. "When do you expect Mr. Kent?"

"In about twenty minutes, Colonel." Sylvester glanced at the wall clock. "Won't you sit down?"

McIntyre took the chair and planted it by the window. Never a very patient man, he waited for Kent with increasing irritation, and at the end of half an hour his temper was uppermost. "Give me something to write with," he demanded of Sylvester. Accepting the clerk's fountain pen without thanks, he walked over to the center table and, drawing out his leather wallet, took from it a visiting card and, stooping over, wrote:

You have but thirty-six hours remaining.   McIntyre.

"See that Mr. Kent gets this card," he directed. "No, don't put it there," irascibly, as the clerk laid the card on top of a pile of letters. "Take it into Mr. Kent's office and put it on his desk."

There was that about Colonel McIntyre which inspired complete obedience to his wishes, and Sylvester followed his directions without further question.

As the clerk stepped into Kent's office McIntyre saw a woman sitting by the empty desk. She turned her head on hearing footsteps and their glances met. A faint exclamation broke from her.

"Margaret!" McIntyre strode past Sylvester. "What are you doing here?'

Mrs. Brewster's ready laugh hid all sign of embarrassment. "Must you know?" she asked archly. "That is hardly fair to Barbara."

"So Barbara sent you here with a message!" Mrs. Brewster treated his remark as a statement and not a question, and briskly changed the subject.

"I can't wait any longer," she pouted. "Please tell Mr. Kent that I am sorry not to have seen him."

"I will, madam." Sylvester placed McIntyre's card in the center of Kent's desk and flew to open the door for Mrs. Brewster.

As the widow stepped into the corridor she brushed by an over-dressed woman, whose cheap finery gave clear indication of her tastes. Hardly noticing another's presence she turned and took McIntyre's arm and they strolled off together, her soft laugh floating back to where Mrs. Sylvester stood talking to her husband.

CHAPTER XIII. THE FACE AT THE WINDOW

Harry Kent rang the doorbell at the McIntyre residence for the fifth time, and wondered what had become of the faithful Grimes; the butler was usually the soul of promptness, and to keep a caller waiting on the doorstep would, in his category, rank as the height of impropriety. As Kent again raised his hand toward the bell, the door swung open suddenly and Barbara beckoned to him to come inside.

"The bell is out of order," she explained. "I saw you from the window. Hurry, and Grimes won't know that you are here," and she darted ahead of him into the reception room. Kent followed more slowly; he was hurt that she had had no other greeting for him.

"Babs, aren't you glad to see me?" he asked wistfully.

For an instant her eyes were lighted by her old sunny smile.

"You know I am," she whispered softly. As his arms closed around her and their lips met in a tender kiss she added fervently, "Oh, Harry, why didn't you make me marry you in the happy bygone days?"

"I asked you often enough," he declared.

"Will you go with me to Rockville at once?" Her face changed and she drew back from him. "No," she said. "It is selfish of me to think of my own happiness now."

"How about mine?" demanded Kent with warmth. "If you won't consider yourself, consider me."

"I do." She looked out of the window to conceal sudden blinding tears. There was a hint of hidden tragedy in her lovely face which went to Kent's heart.

"Sweetheart," his voice was very tender, "is there nothing I can do for you?"

"Nothing," she shook her head drearily. "This family must 'dree its weir.'"

Kent studied her in silence; that she was in deadly earnest he recognized, she was no hysterical fool or given to sentimental twaddle.

"You came to me on Wednesday to ask my aid in solving Jimmie Turnbull's death," he said. "I have learned certain facts--"

Barbara sprang to her feet. "Wait," she cautioned. "Let me close the door. Now, go on--" with her customary impetuosity she reseated herself.

"Before I do so, I must tell you, Babs, that I recognized the fraud you and Helen perpetrated at the coroner's inquest yesterday afternoon."

"Fraud?"

"Yes," quietly. "I am aware that you impersonated Helen on the witness stand and vice versa. You took a frightful risk."

"I don't see why," she protested. "In my testimony I told nothing but the truth."

"I never doubted you told the truth regarding the events of Monday night as you saw them, but the coroner's questions were put to you under the impression that you were Helen." Kent scrutinized her keenly. "Would Helen have been able to give the same answers that you did without perjuring herself?"

Barbara started and her face paled. "Are you insinuating that Helen killed Jimmie?" she cried.

"No," his emphatic denial was prompt. "But I do believe that she knows more of what transpired Monday night than she is willing to admit. Is that not so, Barbara?"

"Yes," she acknowledged reluctantly.

"Does she know who poisoned Jimmie?"

"No--no!" Barbara rested a firm hand on his shoulder. "I swear Helen does not know. You must believe me, Harry."

"She may not know," Kent spoke slowly. "But are you sure she does not suspect some one?"

"Well, what if I do?" asked Helen quietly, and Kent, looking around, found her standing just inside the door. Her entrance had been noiseless.

"You should tell the authorities, Helen." Kent rose as she passed him and selected a seat which brought her face somewhat in shadow. "If you do not you may retard justice."

"But if I speak I may involve the innocent," she retorted. "I--" her eyes shifted from him to Barbara and back again. "I cannot undertake that responsibility."

"Better that than let the guilty escape through your silence," protested Kent. "Possibly the theories of the police may coincide with yours.

"What are they?" asked Barbara impetuously.

Kent considered before replying. If Detective Ferguson had gone so far as to secure a search warrant to go through Rochester's apartment and office it would not be long before the fact of his being a "suspect" would be common property; there could, therefore, be no harm in his repeating Ferguson's conversation to the twins. In fact, as their legal representative, they were entitled to know the latest developments from him.

"Detective Ferguson believes that the poison was administered by Philip Rochester," he said finally, and watched to see how the announcement would affect them. Barbara's eyes opened to their widest extent, and back in her corner, into which she had gradually edged her chair, Helen emitted a long, long breath as her taut muscles relaxed.

"What makes Ferguson think Philip guilty?" demanded Barbara.

"It is known that he and Jimmie were not on good terms," replied Kent. "Then Rochester's disappearance after Jimmie's death lends color to the theory."

"Has Philip really disappeared?" asked Helen. "You showed me a telegram--"

"Apparently the telegram was a fake," admitted Kent. "The Cleveland police report that he is not at the address given in the telegram."

"But who could have an object in sending such a telegram?" asked Barbara slowly.

"Rochester, in the hope of throwing the police off his track, if he really killed Jimmie." Kent looked straight at Helen. "It was while searching our office safe for trace of Rochester's present address that Ferguson obtained possession of your sealed envelope."

Helen plucked nervously at the ribbon on her gown. "Did the detective open the envelope" she asked.

"No."

"Are you sure?"

"Positive; the red seal was unbroken."

"Tell us how the envelope came to be stolen from you," coaxed Barbara.

"We were in the little smoking porch off the dining room at the Club de Vingt." Barbara smiled her remembrance of it, and motioned Kent to continue. "Ferguson had just put down the envelope on the table and I started to pick it up when cheering in the dining room distracted my attention and I, with the others, went to see what it was about. When I returned to the porch the envelope was no longer on the table."

"Who were with you?" questioned Helen.

"Your father, Mrs. Brewster--"

"Of course," murmured Barbara. "Go on, Harry."

"Detective Ferguson and Ben Glymer," Barbara made a wry face, "and"--went on Kent, not heeding her, "each of these persons deny any further knowledge of the envelope, except they declare it was lying on the table when we all made a dash for the dining room.

"Who was the last to leave the porch?" asked Helen.

"Ben Clymer."

"And he saw no one take the envelope?"

"He declares that he had his back to the table, part of the time, but to the best of his knowledge no one took the envelope."

"One of them must have," insisted Barbara.

"The envelope hadn't legs or wings."

"One of them did take it," agreed Kent.

"But which one is the question. Frankly, to find the answer, I must know the contents of the envelope, Helen."

"Why?"

"Because then I will have some idea who would be enough interested in the envelope to steal it."

Helen considered him long and thoughtfully. "I cannot answer your question," she announced finally. She saw his face harden, and hastened to explain. "Not through any lack of confidence in you, Harry, b-b-but," she stumbled in her speech. "I--I do not know what the envelope contains."

Kent stared at her open-mouthed. "Then who requested you to lock the envelope in Rochester's safe?" he demanded, and receiving no reply, asked suddenly: "Was it Rochester?"

"I am not at liberty to tell you," she responded; her mouth set in obstinate lines and before he could press his request a second time, she asked: "Philip Rochester defended Jimmie in court when every one thought him a burglar; why then should Philip have picked him out to attack--he is not a homicidal maniac?"

"No, but the police contend that Rochester recognized Jimmie in his make-up and decided to kill him; hoping his death would be attributed to angina pectoris, and no post-mortem held," wound up Kent.

"I don t quite understand"--Helen raised her handkerchief to her forehead and removed a drop of moisture. "How did Philip kill Jimmie there in court before us all?"

"Ferguson believes that he put the dose of aconitine in the glass of water which Jimmie asked for," explained Kent, and would have continued his remarks, but a scream from Barbara startled him.

"There, look at the window," she cried. "I saw a face peering in. Look quick, Harry, look!"

Kent needed no second bidding, but although he craned his head far outside the open window and gazed both up and down the street and along the path to the kitchen door, he failed to see any one. "Was it a man or woman?" he asked, turning back to the room.

"I--I couldn't tell; it was just a glimpse." Barbara stood resting one hand on the table, her weight leaning upon it. Not for words would she have had Kent know that her knees were shaking under her.

"Did you see the face, Helen?" As he put the question Kent looked around at the silent girl in the corner; she had slipped back in her chair and, with closed eyes, lay white-lipped and limp. With a leap Kent gained her side and his hand sought her pulse.

"Ring for brandy and water," he directed as Barbara came to his aid. "Helen has fainted."

Twenty minutes later Kent hastened out of the McIntyre house and, turning into Connecticut Avenue, boarded a street car headed south. After carrying Helen to the twins' sitting room he had assisted Barbara in reviving her. He had wondered at the time why Barbara had not summoned the servants, then concluded that neither sister wished a scene. That Helen was worse than she would admit he appreciated, and advised Barbara to send for Dr. Stone. The well-meant suggestion had apparently fallen on deaf ears, for no physician had appeared during the time he was in the house, nor had Barbara used the telephone, almost at her elbow as she sat by her sister's couch, to summon Dr. Stone. Kent had only waited long enough to convince himself that Helen was out of danger, and then had departed.

It was nearly one o'clock when he finally stepped inside his office, and he found his clerk and a dressy female bending eagerly over a newspaper. They looked up at his approach and Sylvester came forward.

"This is my wife, sir," he explained, and Kent bowed courteously to Mrs. Sylvester. "We were just reading this account of Mr. Rochester's disappearance; it's dreadful, sir, to think that the police believe him guilty of Mr. Turnbull's murder."

"Dreadful, indeed," agreed Kent; the news had been published even sooner than he had imagined. "What paper is that?"

"The noon edition of the Times." Sylvester handed it to him.

"Thanks," Kent flung down his hat and spread open the paper. "Who have been here to-day?"

"Colonel McIntyre, sir; he left a card for you." Sylvester hurried into Kent's office, to return a moment later with a visiting card. "He left this, sir, for you with most particular directions that it be handed to you at once on your arrival."

Kent read the curt message on the card without comment and tore the pasteboard into tiny bits.

"Any one else been in this morning?" he asked.

"Yes, sir." Sylvester consulted a written memorandum. "Mr. Black called, also Colonel Thorne, Senator Harris, and Mrs. Brewster."

"Mrs. Brewster!" The newspaper slipped from Kent's fingers in his astonishment. "What did she want here?"

"To see you, sir, so she said, but she first asked for Mr. Rochester," explained Sylvester, stooping over to pick up the inside sheet of the Times which had separated from the others. "I told her that Mr. Rochester was unavoidably detained in Cleveland; then she said she would consult you and I let her wait in your office for the good part of an hour."

Kent thought a moment then walked toward his door; on its threshold he paused, struck by a sudden idea.

"Did Colonel McIntyre come with Mrs. Brewster?" he asked.

"No, Mr. Kent; he came in while she was here."

"And they went off together," volunteered Mrs. Sylvester, who had been a silent listener to their conversation. Kent started; he had forgotten the woman. "Excuse me, Mr. Kent," she continued, and stepped toward him. "I presume, likely, that you are very interested in this charge of murder against your partner, Mr. Rochester."

"I am," affirmed Kent, as Mrs. Sylvester paused.

"I am too, sir," she confided to him. "Cause you see I was in the court room when Mr. Turnbull died and I'm naturally interested."

"Naturally," agreed Kent with a commiserating glance at his clerk; the latter's wife threatened to be loquacious, and he judged from her looks that it was a habit which had grown with the years. As a general rule he abhorred talkative women, but--"And what took you to the police court on Tuesday morning?"

"Why, me and Mr. Sylvester have our little differences like other married couples," she explained. "And sometimes we ask the Court to settle them." She caught Kent's look of impatience and hurried her speech. "The burglar case came on just after ours was remanded, and seeing the McIntyre twins, whom I've often read about, I just thought I'd stay. Let me have that paper a minute."

"Certainly," Kent gave her the newspaper and she ran her finger down the columns devoted to the Turnbull case with a slowness that set his already excited nerves on edge.

"Here's what I'm looking for," she exclaimed triumphantly, a minute later, and pointed to the paragraph:

> "Mrs. Margaret Perry Brewster, the fascinating widow, added
>   nothing material to the case in her testimony, and she was
>   quickly excused, after stating that she was told about the tragedy
> by the McIntyre twins upon their return from the
>   Police Court."

"Well what of it?" asked Kent.

"Only this, Mr. Kent;" Mrs. Sylvester enjoyed nothing so much as talking to a good looking man, especially in the presence of her husband, and she could not refrain from a triumphant look at him as she went on with her remarks. "There was a female sitting on the bench next to me in Court; in fact, she and I were the only women on that side, and I kinder noticed her on that account, and then I saw she was all done up in veils--I couldn't see her face.

"I caught her peering this way and that during the burglar's hearing; I don't reckon she could see well through all the veils. Now, don't get impatient, Mr. Kent; I'm getting to my point--that woman sitting next to me in the police court was the widow Brewster."

"What!" Kent laughed unbelievingly. "Oh, come, you are mistaken."

"I am not, sir." Mrs. Sylvester spoke with conviction. "Now, why does Mrs. Brewster declare at the coroner's inquest that she only heard of the Turnbull tragedy from the McIntyre twins on their return home?"

"You must be mistaken," argued Kent.

"Why, you admit yourself that the woman was so swathed in veils that you could not see her face."

"No, but I heard her laugh in court," Mrs. Sylvester spoke in deep earnestness and Kent placed faith in her statement in spite of his outward skepticism. "And I heard her laugh in this corridor this morning and I placed her as the same woman. I asked Mr. Sylvester who she was, and he told me. I'd been reading this account of the Turnbull inquest, and I recollected seeing Mrs. Brewster's name, and my husband and I were just reading the account over when you came in."

Kent gazed in perplexity at Mrs. Sylvester. "Why did Mrs. Brewster laugh in the police court?" he asked.

"When Dr. Stone exclaimed to the deputy marshal--'Your prisoner appears ill!'" declared Mrs. Sylvester; she enjoyed the dramatic, and that Kent was hanging on her words she was fully aware, in spite of his expressionless face. "Dr. Stone lifted the burglar in his arms and then Mrs. Brewster laughed as she laughed in the corridor to-day--a soft gurgling laugh."

CHAPTER XIV. PAY CASH

It was the rush hour at the Metropolis Trust Company and the busy paying teller counted out silver and gold and treasury notes of varying denominations with the mechanical precision and exactness which experience gives. Suddenly his hand stopped midway toward the money drawer, his attention arrested by the signature on a check. A swift glance upward showed him a girl's face at the grille of the window. There was an instant's pause, then she addressed him.

"Do hurry, Mr. McDonald; father is waiting for me."

"Pardon me, Miss McIntyre." He stamped the check and laid it to one side, "how do you want the money?"

"Oh, I forgot." She glanced at a memorandum on the back of an envelope. "Mrs.

Brewster wishes ten tens, five twenties, and ten ones. Thank you, good afternoon," and counting over the money she thrust it inside her bag and hurried away.

She had been gone a bare five minutes when Kent reached the window and pushed several checks toward the teller.

"Is Mr. Clymer in his office, McDonald?" he asked, placing the bank notes given, him in his wallet.

"I'm not sure." The teller glanced around at the clock; the hands stood at ten minutes of three. "It's pretty near closing time, Kent; still, he may be there."

"I'll go and see," and with a nod of farewell Kent turned on his heel and walked off in the direction of the office of the bank president. On reaching there he saw, through the glass partition of the door, Clymer seated in earnest conclave with two men.

Happening to glance up Clymer recognized Kent and beckoned to him to come inside. "You know Taylor," he said by way of introduction. "And this is Mr. Harding of New York--Mr. Kent," he turned around in his swivel chair to face the three men. "Draw up a chair, Kent; we were just going over to see you.

"Yes?" Kent looked inquiringly at the bank president, the gravity of his manner betokened serious tidings. "What is it, Mr. Clymer?"

Clymer did not reply at once. "It's this," he said finally, with blunt directness. "Your partner, Philip Rochester, appears to be a bankrupt. Harding and Taylor came in here to attach his private bank account to cover indebtedness to their business firms."

An exclamation broke from Kent. "Impossible!" he gasped.

"I would have said the same this morning," declared Clymer. "But on investigation I find that Rochester has over-drawn his account here for a large amount and borrowed heavily. The further I look into his financial affairs the more involved I find them."

"But"--Kent was white-lipped. "I know for an absolute fact that Rochester was paid some exceedingly large fees last week, totaling over fifty thousand dollars."

"He has never deposited such a sum, or anywhere like that amount in this bank either last week or this," stated Clymer, running his eyes down a bank statement which, with several pass books, lay on his desk.

"Does he carry accounts at other banks?" inquired Harding.

"Not that I can discover," responded Taylor. "I have been to every national and private banking house in Washington, but all deny having him as a depositor. Did Rochester ever bank out of town, Kent?"

"Not to my knowledge." Kent drew out a bank book. "Here is the firm's balance, Mr. Clymer; we bank here, you know."

"Yes." Clymer's look of anxiety deepened.

"Did you see McDonald as you came in?"

"Yes, he cashed some checks for me."

"Your personal checks?"

"Yes." Kent looked questioningly at Clymer. "What do you mean?"

"Only this; that all moneys deposited here in the firm name of Rochester and Kent have been drawn out."

"That's not possible!" Kent started up.

"Checks on that account must bear both Rochester's signature and mine."

"Checks bearing both signatures have been presented for the total sum deposited to your credit," stated Clymer and he picked up four canceled checks. "See for yourself."

Kent stared at the checks in dumbfounded silence; then carrying them to the light he examined them with minute care before bringing them back to the bank president.

"This is the first I have heard of these transactions," he said.

"You mean--"

"That the signatures are clever forgeries." His statement was heard with gravity. Taylor exchanged a meaning look with the New Yorker.

"You mean your signature is a forgery," he suggested. "Rochester had a peculiar gift of penmanship."

Kent sprang up. "Do you accuse Philip Rochester of signing these checks and inserting my name to them?"

"I do," calmly. "I am not familiar with your signature, Kent, but that Rochester wrote the body of those four checks and put his own signature at the bottom I will swear to in any court of law. To make them valid he had to add your name."

"But, d--mn it, man!" Kent stared in bewilderment at his three companions. "Rochester was honorable and straight-forward--"

"And addicted to drink," put in Harding. "But not a forger," retorted Kent firmly. Harding's only rejoinder was a skeptical smile as he turned to address Clymer.

"So Rochester not only has taken his own money, but withdrawn that belonging to the firm of Rochester and Kent without the knowledge of his junior partner; it looks black, Mr. Clymer," he remarked. "Especially when taken in consideration with his other involved financial transactions."

"Where will we find Rochester, Kent?" asked Taylor, before the bank president could answer the New Yorker.

Kent paused in indecision. What reply could he make without further involving Rochester in trouble? He had not the faintest idea where Rochester was, but to state that he was missing could not but add to the belief that he had made away with all the money he could lay his hands on. The noon edition of the Times had hinted at Rochester's disappearance but had stated they could not get the statement confirmed from Police Headquarters; obviously Harding and Taylor had not seen the newspaper.

Was it just to the men before him to keep them in the dark? If their claims were true, and Kent never doubted that they were, they had already lost money through Rochester's extraordinary behavior. Kent turned sick at the thought of his own loss--his savings swept away. Would Barbara wait for him--was it fair to ask her?

Taylor broke the prolonged silence.

"I met Detective Ferguson on my way here," he stated. "He told me that the police were looking for Rochester."

"What?" Harding looked up, startled. "Why didn't you inform me of that?"

"Well, I thought we'd better hear from Mr. Clymer the true state of Rochester's finances," responded Taylor. "I never anticipated such facts as he has given us."

"But if you knew the police were after Rochester--" objected Harding.

Clymer broke into the conversation; there was a heavy frown on his usually placid countenance. "I judged from Detective Ferguson's confidences to us, Kent, at the Club de Vingt that he was wanted by the police in connection with the Turnbull tragedy, but the facts brought out through Harding's action to attach Rochester's bank account, puts a different construction on Rochester's disappearance."

"What had Rochester to do with Jimmie Turnbull?" questioned Harding, before Kent could answer Clymer.

"They lived together," he replied shortly.

"And one dies and the other disappears," Harding whistled dolefully. "Wasn't Mr. Turnbull an official of this bank, Mr. Clymer?"

"Yes, our cashier."

"Were his affairs involved?"

"Not in the least," Clymer spoke with emphasis. "A most honorable fellow, Jimmie Turnbull; his murder was a shocking affair."

"Have the police found any motive for the crime, Kent?" asked Taylor.

"I believe not."

Harding, who had been ruminating in silence, leaned forward, his expression alight with a sudden idea.

"Could it be that Turnbull found out that Rochester was passing forged checks, and Rochester insured his silence by Poisoning him?" he asked.

Clymer and Kent exchanged glances, as Kent's thoughts reverted to the forged letter presented by Turnbull to the bank's treasurer, whereby he had been given McIntyre's valuable negotiable securities. Could it be that Rochester had written the letter, given it to his room-mate, Turnbull, and the latter, thinking it genuine, had secured the McIntyre securities and handed them over to Rochester? The idea took Kent's breath away; and yet, the more he contemplated it, the more feasible it appeared.

"What's the date on those checks?" demanded Kent.

"Tuesday of this week--the day Jimmie Turnbull died." Clymer turned them over. "They are drawn payable to cash, and bear no endorsement, which shows Rochester must have presented them himself."

Harding and Taylor glanced significantly at each other, but neither spoke. Suddenly Kent pushed back his chair and rose without ceremony.

"Don't go, Kent." Clymer took up some papers. "There's a matter--"

"It will keep." Kent's mouth was set and determined. "I give you my word of honor that all Rochester's honest debts will be paid by the firm if necessary; I will obligate myself to that extent," he paused. "As for you fellows," turning to Harding and Taylor who had also risen. "Give me twenty-four hours--"

"What for?" they chorused.

"To locate Philip Rochester," and waiting for no answer Kent bolted out of the office.

CHAPTER XV. WHEN THE LIGHT FAILED

The city lights were springing up block T after block along Pennsylvania Avenue as Detective Ferguson left that busy thoroughfare and hurried to the Saratoga. He stepped inside the lobby of the apartment house a full minute before his appointment with its manager, and went at once to look him up. Before he could carry out his purpose he was joined by Harry Kent.

"Finley had to go out," the latter explained.

"I told him I would go up to Rochester's apartment with you."

Ferguson thoughtfully caressed his clean-shaven jaw for a second, then came to a rapid decision.

"Lead the way, sir," he said. "I'll follow." Kent found him a silent companion while in the elevator and when walking down the corridor to Rochester's apartment, but once inside the living room, with the outer door tightly closed, Ferguson tossed down his hat and his whole demeanor changed.

"Sit down, Mr. Kent." He selected a chair near Rochester's desk for himself, as Kent found another. "Let's thrash this thing out; are you working with me or against me?"

"Why do you ask?" Kent's surprise at the question was evident.

"Because every time I arrange to examine this apartment or inquire into Rochester's whereabouts you show up." Ferguson's small eyes were trying to out-stare Kent, but the latter's clear gaze did not drop before his. "Are you aiding Philip Rochester in his efforts to elude arrest?"

"I am not," declared Kent emphatically. "What prompts the question?"

"The fact that you are Rochester's partner," Ferguson pointed out; his manner was still stiff. "It would be only natural for you to help him disappear out of friendship, or"--with a sidelong glance--"from a desire to hush up a scandal."

"On the contrary I want Rochester found and every bit of evidence against him sifted out and aired," retorted Kent. "Two heads are better than one, Ferguson; let us work together. Rochester must be located within the next twenty-four hours."

Ferguson debated a moment, but Kent's speech as well as his manner indicated his sincerity, and the detective shook off his suspicions. "Have you had any further news of your partner?" he asked.

"No; that is"--recalling the scene in the bank early that afternoon--"nothing that relates to Rochester's present whereabouts. Now, Ferguson, to put your charges against Rochester in concrete form, you believe that he was insanely jealous of Jimmie Turnbull, that he recognized him in the Police Court in his burglar disguise, slipped a dose of aconitine in a glass of water which Turnbull drank, and after declaring that his friend had died from angina pectoris, disappeared. Is that all the case you have against him?"

"At present, yes," admitted the detective cautiously.

"All circumstantial evidence--"

"But it will hold in court--"

"Ah, will it?" questioned Kent. "There's one big flaw in your case, Ferguson; the poison used to kill Turnbull."

"Aconitine?"

"Exactly. Your theory is that Rochester slipped the poison in the glass of water on recognizing Turnbull in the police court; now, it is stretching probability to suppose that Rochester, a strong healthy man, was carrying that drug around in his vest pocket."

Ferguson sat forward in his chair, his eyes glittering. "Do you mean to say that you think the murder of Turnbull was premeditated and not committed on the spur of the moment?" he asked.

"The fact that aconitine was used convinces me of that," answered Kent.

Ferguson thought a moment. "If that is the case," he said, grudgingly, "it sort of squashes the charge against Philip Rochester."

"It would seem to," agreed Kent. "But every shred of evidence I find points to Rochester as the guilty man."

Ferguson edged his chair forward. "What have you discovered?" he demanded eagerly.

"This," Kent spoke with increased earnestness. "That Philip Rochester is apparently a bankrupt, that he has over-drawn his private account at the Metropolis Trust Company, and withdrawn our partnership funds from the same bank."

"Your partnership funds!" echoed the detective, eyeing Kent sharply. "How did you come to let him do that?"

"I was not aware that he had done so until Mr. Clymer told me of the transaction this afternoon," answered Kent.

"You did not know"--Ferguson looked at him in dawning comprehension. "You mean Rochester absconded with the funds?"

"Some one forged my name to checks drawn on the firm's account," Kent continued. "I understood they were made payable to cash and presented by Rochester on the day of Turnbull's death."

Ferguson whistled as a slight vent to his feelings. "So you suspect Rochester of being a forger?" Kent made no reply, and he added; after a moment's deliberation, "What bearing has this discovery on Turnbull's death, aside from Rochester's need of funds to make a clean disappearance?"

"If it is true that Rochester was financially embarrassed and forged checks on the Metropolis Trust Company, it establishes another motive for the killing of Turnbull," argued Kent. "Turnbull was cashier of that bank."

"I see; he may have discovered the forgeries--but hold on." Ferguson checked his rapid speech. "When were these forged checks presented at the bank?"

"Tuesday afternoon."

Ferguson's face fell. "Pshaw! man; that was after Turnbull's death--how could he detect the forgeries?"

Kent did not reply at once; instead, he glanced keenly about the living room. The detective had only switched on one of the reading lamps and the greater part was in shadow. It was a pleasant and home-like room, and Kent was conscious of a keener pang for the loss of Jimmie Turnbull and the disappearance of Philip Rochester, as he gazed around. The lawyer and the bank cashier had been, until that winter, congenial comrades, sharing their business success and their apartment in complete accord; and now a shadow as black as that enveloping the unlighted apartment hung over their good names, threatening one or the other with the charge of forgery and of murder. Kent sighed and turned back to the silent detective.

"I can best answer your question by telling you that the day after Jimmie Turnbull died Mr. Clymer sent for me," he began. "I found Colonel McIntyre with him and was told that the Colonel had lost valuable securities left at the bank. These securities had been given by the treasurer of the bank to Jimmie Turnbull when he presented a letter from Colonel McIntyre instructing the bank to surrender the securities to Jimmie."

"Well?" questioned Ferguson. "Go on, sir."

"That letter was a forgery." Kent sat back and watched the detective's rapidly changing expression. "And no trace has been found of the Colonel's securities, last known to be in the possession of Turnbull."

"Great heavens!" ejaculated Ferguson.

"Which was the forger--Turnbull or Rochester?"

Kent shook a puzzled head. "That is for us to discover," he said soberly. "Colonel McIntyre contends that Turnbull forged the letter and stole the securities, then fearing his guilt would become known, committed still another crime--that of suicide, he could have swallowed a dose of aconitine while at the police court."

"Well, I'll be--blessed!" ejaculated Ferguson. "But if he was the forger how does that square with Rochester's peculiar behavior? The checks bearing your forged signatures were presented, mind you, by Rochester after Turnbull's death?"

"It doesn't square," acknowledged Kent frankly. "There is this to be said for Turnbull: he was the soul of honor, his affairs were found to be in excellent condition, he was drawing a good salary, his investments paying well--he did not need to acquire securities or money by resorting to forgery."

"Whereas Philip Rochester was on the point of bankruptcy," remarked Ferguson. "Do you suppose he forged Colonel McIntyre's letter and gave it to Turnbull, and the latter got the securities from the bank treasurer and handed them over to Rochester in good faith, supposing his room-mate would give the papers to Colonel McIntyre?"

Kent nodded in agreement. "It looks that way to me," he said gloomily. "Philip Rochester stood well in the community, his law practice is large and lucrative, and if it had not been for his periods of idleness and--and"--hesitating--"passion for good living, he would never have run into debt."

"But he got there." Ferguson's laugh was contemptuous. "A desperate man will do anything, Mr. Kent."

"I know," Kent looked dubious. "I would believe him guilty if it were not for the use of aconitine--that shows premeditation on the part of the murderer."

"And why shouldn't Rochester plan Turnbull's murder ahead of the scene in the police court?" argued Ferguson. "Wasn't he living in deadly fear of exposure? If he did not commit the murder, why did he run away? And if he is innocent, why doesn't he come forward and prove it?"

"He may not know that he is suspected of the crime," retorted Kent, rising. "It is for us to find Rochester, and I suggest that we search this apartment thoroughly."

"I have already done so," objected Ferguson. "And there wasn't the faintest clew to his hiding place."

"For all that I am not satisfied." Kent walked over and switched on another light. "When I came here on Wednesday night I had a tussle with some man, but he escaped in the dark without my seeing him. I believe he was Rochester."

"You are probably right." Ferguson crossed the room. "And if he came back once, he may return again. Come ahead," and he plunged into the first bedroom. The two men subjected each room to an exhaustive search, but their labors were their only reward; except for an accumulation of dust, the apartment was undisturbed. They had reached the kitchenette-pantry when the gong over their heads sounded loudly, and Kent, with a muttered exclamation hastened toward the front door of the apartment. Ferguson, intent on studying the "L" of the building as seen from the window, was hardly conscious of his departure, and some seconds elapsed before he turned toward the door. As he gained it, he saw a dark shape dart down the hall. With a bound Ferguson started in pursuit, and the next second grappled with the flying man just as the electric lights went out and they were plunged in darkness.

Suddenly Kent's voice echoed down the hall. "Come here quick, Ferguson!"

There was a note of urgency about his appeal, and Ferguson straining his muscles until the blood pounded in his temples, threw the struggling man into a tufted arm-chair which stood by the entrance to the small dining room, and drawing out his handcuffs, slipped them on securely. "Stay there," Ferguson admonished his prisoner. "Or there will be worse coming to you," and he thrust the muzzle of his revolver against the man's heaving chest to illustrate his meaning; then as Kent called again, he sped down the hall and brought up breathless at the front door. The light was still burning in the corridor, though not very brightly, and he saw Kent hand the grinning messenger boy a shiny quarter. Touching his battered cap the boy went whistling away. "Tell the elevator boy to report that a fuse has burned out in Mr. Rochester's apartment," Ferguson called after him, and the lad waved his hand as he dashed into the elevator.

Paying no attention to the detective's call, Kent showed him a white envelope which bore the simple address:

PHILIP ROCHESTER, ESQ. THE SARATOGA

"It's the identical envelope I found in your safe," declared Ferguson

"And which disappeared last night at the Club de Vingt." Kent turned over the envelope. "See, the red seal."

For a minute the men contemplated the seal with the large distinctive letter "B" in the center.

"Open the letter, sir," Ferguson urged and Kent, his fingers fairly trembling, jerked and tore at the linen incased envelope; the flap ripped away and he opened the envelope--it was empty.

Instinctively the two men glanced down at the parquetry flooring; nothing but a thin coating of dust lay there, and Kent looked up and down the corridor: it was deserted.

"Do you recognize the handwriting?" asked Ferguson.

"No." Kent regarded the envelope in bewilderment. "What shall we do?"

"Do? Call up the Dime Messenger Service and see where the envelope came from; but first come and see my prisoner."

"Your prisoner?" in profound astonishment.

"Yes. I caught him chasing up the hall after you," explained Ferguson as they hurriedly retraced their steps. "I put handcuffs on him and then went to you. Ah, here's the light!"

"The light, yes; but where's your prisoner?" and Kent, who was a trifle in advance of his companion in reaching the dining room, stood aside to let Ferguson pass him.

The detective halted abruptly. The chair into which he had thrust his prisoner was vacant. The man had disappeared.

With one accord Ferguson and Kent advanced close to the chair, and an oath broke from the detective. On the cushion of the chair, still bearing the impress of a human body, lay a pair of shining new handcuffs.

Dazedly Ferguson stooped over and examined them. They were still securely locked. Wheeling around Kent dashed through the door to his right and Ferguson, collecting his wits, searched the rest of the apartment with minute care. Five minutes later he came face to face with Kent in the living room. "Not a trace of any kind," declared Kent. "It's the same as the other night; the man's gone. It's--it's positively uncanny."

Ferguson's face was red from mortification and his exertions combined.

"The fellow must have slipped from the room by that other door and out through the living room as we came down the hail," he said. "Did you shut the door of the apartment, Mr. Kent, before coming down here to look at the prisoner?"

"Yes." Kent led the way back to the dining room. "Did you recognize the man, Ferguson?"

"No." The detective swore softly as he stared about the room. "The lights went out just as I tackled him."

"It was beastly luck that the fuse burned out at that second," groaned Kent. "Fortune was with him in that; but how did the man get free of the handcuffs?" pointing to them still lying in the chair. "We can't attribute that to luck, unless"-- staring keenly at Ferguson--"unless you did not snap them on the man's wrists, after all."

"I did; I swear it," declared Ferguson. "I'm no novice at that business. Here, don't touch them, Mr. Kent," as his companion bent toward the chair. "There may be finger marks on the steel; if so"--he drew out his handkerchief, and taking care not to handle the burnished metal, he folded the handcuffs carefully in it and put them in his coat pocket. "There's no use lingering here, Mr. Kent; this apartment is vacant now except for us. I must get to Headquarters."

"Hadn't you better telephone for an operative and station him here?" suggested Kent.

"I did so while you were searching the back rooms," replied Ferguson. "There," as the gong sounded. "That's Nelson, now."

But the person who stood in the outer corridor when they opened the front door was not Nelson, the operative, but Dr. Stone.

"Can I see Mr. Rochester?" he asked, then catching sight of Kent standing just back of the detective, he added, "Hello, Kent; I thought I heard some one walking about in here from my apartment next door, and concluded Rochester had returned. Can I see him?"

"N-no," Kent spoke slowly, with a side-glance at the silent detective. "Rochester has been here--and left."

CHAPTER XVI. THE CRIMSON OUTLINE

Barbara McIntyre made the round of the library for the fifth time, testing each of the seven doors opening into it to see that they ere closed behind their portieres, then she turned back to her sister, who sat cross-logged before a small safe.

"Any luck?" she asked

Instead of replying Helen removed the key from the lock of the steel door and regarded it attentively. The safe was of an obsolete pattern and in place of the customary combination lock, was opened by means of a key, unique in appearance.

"It is certainly the key which father mislaid six months ago," she declared. "Grimes found it just after father had a new key made and gave it to me. And yet I can't get the door open."

"Let me try." Barbara crouched down by her sister and inserted the key again in the lock, but her efforts met with no results, and after five minutes' steady manipulation she gave up the attempt. "I am afraid it is impossible," she admitted. "Seems to me I have heard that the lost key will not open a safe after a new key has been supplied."

Helen rose slowly to her feet, stretching her cramped limbs carefully as she did so, and sank down in the nearest chair. Her attitude indicated dejection.

"Then we can't find the envelope," she muttered. "Hurry, Babs, and close the outer door; father may return at any moment."

Barbara obeyed the injunction with such alacrity that the door, concealing the space in the wall where stood the safe, flew to with a bang and the twins jumped nervously.

"Take care!" exclaimed Helen sharply. "Do you wish to arouse the household?"

"No danger of that." But Barbara glanced apprehensively about the library in spite of her reassuring statement. "The servants are either out or upstairs, and Margaret Brewster is writing letters in our sitting room."

"Hadn't you better go upstairs and join her?" Helen suggested. "Do, Babs," as her sister hesitated. "I cannot feel sure that she will not interrupt us."

"But my joining her won't keep Margaret upstairs," objected Barbara.

"No, but you can call and warn me if she is on her way down, and that will give me time to--to straighten father's papers," going over to a large carved table littered with magazines, letters, and silver ornaments. Her sister did not move, and she glanced at her with an irritated air, very foreign to her customary manner. "Go, Barbara."

The curt command brought a stare from Barbara, but it did not accelerate her halting footsteps; instead she moved with even greater slowness toward the hall door; her active brain tormented with an unspoken and unanswered question. Why was Helen so anxious for her departure? She had accepted her offer of assistance in her search of the library with such marked reluctance that Barbara had marveled at the time, and now...

"Are you quite sure, Helen, that father had the envelope in his pocket this morning?" she asked for the third time since the search began.

"He had an envelope--I caught a glimpse of the red seal," answered Helen. "Then, just before dinner he was putting some papers in the safe. Oh, if Grimes had only come in a moment sooner to announce dinner, I might have had a chance to look in the safe before father closed the door."

Whatever reply Barbara intended making was checked by the rattling of the knob of the hall door; it turned slowly, the door opened and, pushing aside the portieres drawn across the entrance, Margaret Brewster glided in. "So glad to find you," she cooed. "But why have you closed up the room and turned on all the lights?"

"To see better," retorted Barbara promptly as the widow's eyes roved around the large room, taking silent note of the drawn curtains and portieres, and the somewhat disarranged furniture. "Come inside, Margaret, and help us in our search."

"For what?" The widow tried to keep her tone natural, but a certain shrill alertness crept into it and Barbara, who was watching her closely, was quick to detect the change. Helen's color altered at the question, and she observed the widow's entrance with veiled hostility.

"For my seal," Barbara answered. "The one with the big letter 'B.' Have you seen it?"

"I?--No." The widow took a chair uninvited near Helen. "You look tired, Helen dear; why don't you go to bed?"

"I could not sleep if I did." Helen passed a nervous finger across her eyes. "But don't let me keep you and Babs up; it won't take me long to arrange to-morrow's market order for Grimes."

Under pretense of searching for pencil and paper Helen contrived to see the address of every letter lying on the table, but the envelope she sought, with its red seal, was not among them. When she looked up again, pencil and paper in hand, she found Mrs. Brewster leaning lazily back and regarding her from under half-closed lids. "You are very like your father, Helen," she commented softly.

The girl stiffened. "Am I? Babs and I are generally thought to resemble our mother."

"In appearance, yes; but I mean mannerisms--for instance, the way of holding your pencil, your handwriting, even, closely resembles your father's." Mrs. Brewster pointed to the notes Helen was scribbling on the paper and to an open letter bearing Colonel McIntyre's signature at the bottom of the sheet lying beside the pad to illustrate her meaning. "These are almost identical."

"You are a close observer." Helen completed her memorandum and laid it aside. "What became of father?"

"He went to a stag supper at the Willard," chimed in Barbara, stopping her aimless walk about the library. "He said we were not to wait up for him."

Helen pushed back her chair and rose with some abruptness.

"I am more tired than I realized," she remarked and involuntarily stretched her weary muscles. "Come, Margaret," laying a persuasive hand on the widow's shoulder. "Be a trump and rub my forehead with cologne as you used to do abroad when I had a headache. It always put me to sleep then; and, oh, how I long for sleep now!"

There was infinite pathos in her voice and Mrs. Brewster sprang up and threw her arm about her in ready sympathy.

"You poor darling!" she exclaimed. "Let me put you to bed; Mammy taught me the art of soothing frayed nerves. Come with us, Babs," holding out her left hand to

Barbara. But the latter, with a dexterous twist, slipped away from her touch.

"I must stay and straighten the library," she announced.

Mrs. Brewster's delicate color had deepened. "It would be as well to open some of the doors," she agreed coldly. "The library looks odd, not to say funereal," she glanced down the spacious room and shivered ever so slightly. "Do, Babs, put out some of the lights; they are blinding."

"Oh, I'll turn them all out"--Barbara sought the electric switch.

"But your father--"

"No need to worry about father; he can find his way about in the dark like a cat," responded Barbara with unabated cheerfulness. "Seems to me, Margaret, you and father are getting mighty chummy these days."

The sudden darkness into which Barbara's impatient fingers, pressing against the electric light buttons, plunged the library and its occupants, prevented her seeing the curious glance which Mrs. Brewster shot at her. Helen, who had listened to their chatter with growing impatience, looked back over her shoulder.

"Hurry, Barbara, and come upstairs. Now, Margaret," and she piloted the widow along the hall toward the staircase without giving her an opportunity to answer Barbara's last remark. Barbara, pausing only long enough to pull back the portieres of the hall door and arrange them as they hung customarily, turned to go upstairs just as Grimes came down the hall from the dining room carrying a large tray with pitchers of ice water and glasses.

"I thought you had gone to your room, Grimes," she remarked, as the butler waited respectfully for her to pass him.

"I've just come in, miss, and found Murray had left the tray in the dining room," explained Grimes hurriedly. "I hope, miss, I'll not disturb the ladies by knocking at their doors now with this ice water."

"Oh, no, Mrs. Brewster and Miss Helen have only just gone upstairs." Barbara paused in front of the butler and poured out a glass of water. "I can't wait, Grimes, I am too thirsty."

"Certainly, miss, that's all right." Grimes craned his head around and looked up and down the hail, then leaning over he placed the tray on a convenient table and stepped close to Barbara.

"I've been reading the newspapers very carefully, miss," he began, taking care to keep his voice lowered. "Especially that part of Mr. Turnbull's inquest which tells about the post-mortem."

"Well, what then?" asked Barbara quickly as the butler paused and again glanced up and down the hall.

"Just this, miss," he spoke almost in a whisper. "The doctors do say poor Mr. Turnbull was poisoned by acca--aconitine," stumbling over the word. "It's a curious thing, miss, that I brought some of that very drug into this house last Sunday."

"You did!" Barbara's fresh young voice rose in astonishment.

"Hush, miss!" The butler raised both hands. "Hush!" He glanced cautiously around, then continued. "Colonel McIntyre sent me to the druggist with a prescription from Dr. Stone for Mrs. Brewster when she had romantic neuralgia."

"Had what?" Barbara looked puzzled, then giggled, but her mirth quickly altered to seriousness at sight of the butler's expression. "Mrs. Brewster had a touch of rheumatic neuralgia the first of the month; do you refer to that?"

"Yes, miss." Grimes spoke more rapidly, but kept his voice lowered. "The druggist told me what the pills were when I exclaimed at their size--regular little pellets, no bigger than that," he demonstrated the size with the tip of his little finger, and would have added more but the gong over the front door rang out with such suddenness that both he and Barbara started violently.

"Just a moment, miss," and he hurried to the front bell, to return after a brief colloquy with a messenger boy, bearing a letter. "It's for Mrs. Brewster, miss," he explained, as Barbara held out her hand.

"I'll give it to her and this also," Barbara took the envelope and a small ice pitcher and glass. "Good night, Grimes. Oh," she stopped midway up the staircase and waited for the butler to overtake her, "Grimes, to whom did you give the aconitine on Sunday?"

"I didn't give it to nobody, miss." The butler was a trifle short of breath; his years did not permit him to keep pace with the twins. "I was in a great hurry as the druggist kept me waiting, and I had to serve tea at once."

"But what did you do with the aconitine pills?" demanded Barbara.

"I left the box on the hall table, miss--"

"Great heavens!" Barbara stared at the butler, then without a word she raced up the staircase and disappeared through the open door of Mrs. Brewster's bedroom.

The light from the hall shone through the transom and doorway in sufficient volume to clearly indicate the different pieces of furniture, and Barbara put the pitcher and glass on the bed stand and laid the letter which Grimes had given her on the dressing table, then went slowly into her own bedroom. She could hear voices, which she recognized as those of her sister and Mrs. Brewster, coming from Helen's bedroom, but absorbed in her own thoughts she undressed in the dark and crept into bed just as Mrs. Brewster passed down the hallway and entered her own room. The widow had taken off her evening gown and slippers and donned a becoming wrapper before she discovered the letter lying on the dresser. Drawing up a chair she dropped into it, let down her long dark hair, and settled back in luxuriant comfort against the tufted upholstery before she ran her well-manicured finger under the flap of the envelope. A slip of paper fell into her lap as she took out the contents of the envelope and she let it rest there while scanning the closely typewritten lines on the Metropolis Trust Company stationery.

Dear Mrs. Brewster, she read. Our bank teller, Mr. McDonald, has questioned the genuineness of the signature on the inclosed check. An important business engagement prevents my calling to-night, but please stop at the bank early to-morrow morning.

I feel that you would prefer to have a personal investigation made rather than have us place the matter in the hands of the police.

Yours faithfully,

BENJAMIN A. CLYMER.

The widow read the note a number of times, then bethinking herself, she picked up the canceled check still lying in her lap, and turned it over. Long and intently she studied the signature--the peculiarly characteristic formation of the letter "B" caught and held her attention. As the seconds ticked themselves into minutes she sat immovable, her face as white as the hand on which she had bowed her head.

Across the hall Helen McIntyre tossed from one side to the other in her soft bed; her restless longing to get up was growing stronger and stronger. While Mrs. Brewster's deft fingers and the cooling cologne had stopped the throbbing in her temples, they had brought only temporary relief in their train and not the sleep which Helen craved. She strained her ears to discover the time by the ticking of her clock, but either it was between the half or quarters of an hour, or it had stopped, for no chimes sounded. With a gasp of exasperation, Helen flung back the bed clothes and sat up. Switching on the light by the side of her bed she hunted for a book, but not finding any, she contemplated for a short space of time a pair of rubber-heeled shoes just showing themselves under the edge of a chair. With sudden decision she left the bed and dressed rapidly. It was not until she had put on her rubber-heeled shoes that she paused. Her hesitation, however, was but brief. Stepping to the bureau, she pulled out a lower drawer and running her hand inside, touched a concealed spring. From the cavity thus exposed she took a small automatic pistol, and with a stealthy glance about her, crept from the room.

The library had been vacant fully an hour when a mouse, intent on making a raid on the candy which Barbara had carelessly left lying loose on one of the tables, paused as a faint creaking sound broke the stillness, then as the noise increased, the mouse scurried back to its hole. The noise resembled the turning of rusty hinges and the soft thud of one piece of wood striking another. There was a strained silence, then, from out of the darkness appeared a tiny stream of light directed full on a white envelope bearing a large red seal.

The next instant the envelope was plucked from the hand holding it, and a figure lay crumpled on the floor from the blow of a descending weapon.

It was closely approaching one o'clock in the morning before Mrs. Brewster stirred from her comfortable bedroom chair. Taking up her electric torch, which she kept always by the side of her bed, she walked quickly down the staircase and into the pitch dark library. Directing her torch-light so that she steered a safe course among the chairs and tables, she approached one of the pieces of carved Venetian furniture and reached out her hand to touch a trap-door. As she looked for the spring she was horrified to see a thin stream of blood oozing through the carving until, reaching the letter "B," it outlined that initial in sinister red.

Scream after scream broke from Mrs. Brewster. She was swaying upon her feet by the time Colonel McIntyre and his daughter Helen reached the library.

"Margaret! What is it?" McIntyre demanded. "Calm yourself, my darling."

The frenzied woman shook off his soothing hand.

"See, see!" she cried and pointed with her torch.

"She means the Venetian casket," explained Helen, who had paused before joining them to switch on the light.

Colonel McIntyre gazed in amazement at the piece of furniture; then catching sight of the blood-stain, he raised the small trap-door or peep hole, in the top of the oblong box which stood breast high, supported on a beautifully carved base.

There was a breathless pause; then McIntyre unceremoniously jerked the electric torch from Mrs. Brewster's nervous fingers and turned its rays of the interior of the casket. Stretched at full length lay the figure of a man, and from a wound in his temple flowed a steady stream of blood.

"Good God!" McIntyre staggered back against Helen. "Grimes!"

CHAPTER XVII. A QUESTION OF HOUSE-BREAKING

The genial president of the Metropolis Trust Company was late. Mrs. Brewster, waiting in his well-appointed office, restrained her ill-temper only by an exertion of will-power. She detested being kept waiting, and that morning she had many errands to attend to before the luncheon hour.

"May I use your telephone?" she asked Mr. Clymer's secretary, and the young man rose with alacrity from his desk. Mrs. Brewster never knew what it was to lack attention, even her own sex were known on occasions to give her gowns and, (what captious critics termed her "frivolous conduct") undivided attention.

"Can I look up the number for you?" the secretary asked as Mrs. Brewster took up the telephone book and fumbled for the gold chain of her lorgnette.

"Oh, thank you," her smile showed each pretty dimple. "I wish to speak to Mr. Kent, of the firm of Rochester and Kent."

"Harry Kent?" The young secretary dropped the book without looking at it, and gave a number to the operator, and then handed the instrument to Mrs. Brewster.

"Mr. Kent not in, did you say?" asked the widow. "Who is speaking? Ah, Mr. Sylvester--has Mr. Rochester returned?---Both partners away"... she paused... "I'll call later--Mrs. Brewster, good morning."

Mrs. Brewster hung up the receiver and turned to the secretary.

"I don't believe I can wait any longer," she began, and paused, as Benjamin Clymer appeared in the doorway.

"So sorry to be late," he exclaimed, shaking her hand warmly. "And I am sorry, also, to have called you here on such an errand."

Mrs. Brewster waited until the young secretary had withdrawn out of earshot before replying; then taking the chair Clymer placed for her near his own, she opened her gold mesh bag and took out a canceled check and laid it on the desk in front of the bank president.

"Your bank honored this check?" she asked.

"Yes."

"Who presented it?"

Clymer pressed the buzzer and his secretary came at once.

"Ask Mr. McDonald to step here," and as the man vanished on his errand, he addressed Mrs. Brewster. "How is Colonel McIntyre this morning?"

Mrs. Brewster's eyes opened at the question. "Quite well," she replied, and prompted by her curiosity added: "What made you think him ill?"

"I stopped at Dr. Stone's office on the way down town, and his boy told me the doctor had been sent for by Colonel McIntyre," Clymer explained. "I hope neither of the twins is ill."

"No. Colonel McIntyre sent for Dr. Stone to attend Grimes--"

"The butler! Too bad he is ill; Grimes is an institution in the McIntyre household." Clymer spoke with sincere regret, and Mrs. Brewster eyed him approvingly; she liked good-looking men of his stamp. "Come in, McDonald," as the bank teller appeared. "You know Mrs. Brewster?"

"Mr. McDonald was one of my first acquaintances in Washington," and Mrs. Brewster smiled as she held out her hand.

"About this check, McDonald," Clymer handed it to the teller as he spoke. "Who presented it?"

"Miss McIntyre."

"Which Miss McIntyre?" Mrs. Brewster put the question with swift intentness.

"I can't tell one twin from the other," confessed McDonald. "But as you see, the check is made payable to Barbara McIntyre."

"The inference being that Barbara McIntyre presented the check for payment," commented Clymer, and McDonald bowed. "It would seem, therefore, that Barbara wrote your signature on the check, Mrs. Brewster."

"No." The widow had whitened under her rouge, but her eyes did not falter in their direct gaze. "The signature is genuine. I drew the check."

The two men exchanged glances. The bank president was the first to break the short silence. "In that case there is nothing more to be said," he remarked, and picking up the check handed it to Mrs. Brewster. Without a glance at it, she folded the paper and placed it inside her gold mesh bag.

"I must not take up any more of your time," she said. "I thank you--both."

"Mrs. Brewster." Clymer spoke impulsively. "I'd like to shake hands with you."

Coloring warmly, the widow slipped her small hand inside his, and with a friendly bow to McDonald, she walked through the bank, keeping up with Clymer's long strides as best she could. As they crossed the sidewalk to the waiting limousine they ran almost into the arms of Harry Kent, whose rapid gait did not suit the congested condition of the "Wall Street" of Washington. "I tried to reach you on the telephone this morning," exclaimed Mrs. Brewster, after greeting him.

"So my clerk informed me when I saw him a few minutes ago." Kent helped her inside the limousine. "Won't you come to my office now?"

"But that will be taking you from Mr. Clymer," remonstrated Mrs. Brewster. "Weren't you on the way to the bank?"

"I was," admitted Kent. "But I can see Mr. Clymer later in the day."

"And I'll be less occupied then," added Clymer. "Go with Mrs. Brewster, Kent; good morning, madam," and with a courtly bow Clymer withdrew.

Kent's office was only around the corner, and as Mrs. Brewster kept up a running fire of impersonal gossip, Kent had no opportunity to satisfy his curiosity regarding her reasons for wanting to interview him. As the limousine drew up at the curb in front of his office, a man darting down the steps of the building, caught sight of Kent and hurried to the car window.

"I was just trying to catch you at the bank, Mr. Kent," he explained, and looking around Kent recognized Sylvester. "There's been three telephone calls for you in succession from Colonel McIntyre to hurry to his home."

"Thanks, Sylvester." Kent turned to Mrs. Brewster. "Would you mind driving me to the McIntyre? We can talk on the way there."

Mrs. Brewster picked up the speaking tube. "Home, Harris," she directed, as the chauffeur listened for the order.

Neither spoke as the big car started up the street but as they swung past old St. John's Church, Mrs. Brewster broke her silence.

"Mr. Kent," she drew further back in her corner. "I claim a woman's privilege--to change my mind. Forget that I ever expressed a wish to consult you professionally, and remember, I am always glad to meet you as a friend."

"Certainly, Mrs. Brewster, as you wish." Kent's tone, expressing polite acquiescence, covered mixed feelings. What had caused the widow to change her mind so suddenly, and above all, what had she wished to consult him about? He faced her more directly. She was charmingly gowned, and in spite of his perplexities, he could not but admire her air of quiet elegance and the soft dark eyes regarding him in friendly good-fellowship. Suddenly realizing that his glance had become a fixed stare, he hastily averted his eyes from her face, catching sight, as he did so, of the gold mesh bag lying in her lap. The glint of sunlight brought into prominence the handsomely engraved letter "B" on its surface. An unexpected swerve of the limousine, as the chauffeur turned short to avoid a speeding army truck, caused both Kent and Mrs. Brewster to sway forward and the gold mesh bag slid to the floor, carrying with it the widow's handkerchief and gold vanity box. Kent stooped over and picked up the articles as well as the contents of the mesh bag, which had opened in its descent and spilled her money and papers over the floor of the limousine.

"Oh, thank you," exclaimed Mrs. Brewster, as he handed her the bag, box, and bank notes. "Don't bother to look for that quarter; Harris will find it at the garage."

Kent ignored her remark as he again searched the floor of the car; he was glad of the pretext to avoid looking at the widow. He wanted time to collect his thoughts for, in Picking up her belongings, her handkerchief had caught his attention--he had seen its mate in the possession of Detective Ferguson, and clinging to it the broken portions of the capsules of amyl nitrite which Jimmie Turnbull had inhaled just before his mysterious death.

Into Kent's mind flashed Mrs. Sylvester's statement that Mrs. Brewster was in the police court at the time of the tragedy, although in her testimony at the inquest she had sworn she had not heard of Jimmie's death until the return of Helen and Barbara McIntyre. She had been in the police court, and Jimmie had used her handkerchief--a mate to the one she was then holding, the letter "B" with its peculiar twist was unmistakable--and "B" stood for Brewster as well as for Barbara! Kent drew in his breath sharply.

"My handkerchief, please," the widow held out her hand, and after a moment's hesitation, Kent gave it to her.

"Pardon me," he apologized. "I was struck by the handkerchief's appearance."

Mrs. Brewster turned it over. "In what way is the handkerchief unique?" she asked, laughing.

"Because Jimmie Turnbull crushed amyl nitrite capsules in its mate just before he died," explained Kent quietly. "Detective Ferguson claims that Jimmie unintentionally broke more than one capsule in the handkerchief, was overcome by the powerful fumes and died."

"But the inquest proved that Jimmie was killed by a dose of aconitine poison," she reminded him, as she tucked the handkerchief up her sleeve.

Kent did not reply immediately. "A man does not usually carry a woman's handkerchief about with him," he commented slowly. "Odd, is it not, that Jimmie should have used a handkerchief of yours in the police court just prior to his death, while you were sitting a few feet away?"

"I?" Mrs. Brewster turned and regarded him steadfastly. She was deadly white under her rouge. "Mr. Kent, are you crazy?"

"Yes, crazy to know why you kept your presence in the police court on Tuesday morning a secret," replied Kent. In their earnestness neither noticed Kent's absent-minded clutch on a small folded paper which he had picked up from the floor of the limousine. "Mrs. Brewster, why did you laugh when Dr. Stone carried Jimmie Turnbull out of the court room?"

Mrs. Brewster sat still in her corner of the car; so still that Kent, observing her closely, feared that she had fainted. She had dropped her eyes, and her face, set like marble, gave him no key to her thoughts.

The door of the limousine was jerked open almost before the car came to a full stop in front of the McIntyre residence, and Colonel McIntyre offered his hand to help Mrs. Brewster out. On the step she turned to Kent, who had lifted his hat to McIntyre in silent greeting.

"Your forte lies as a romancer rather than a lawyer, Mr. Kent," she said, and not giving him time for a reply, almost ran inside the house.

"Glad you could get here so soon, Kent," remarked McIntyre, signing to his chauffeur to drive on before he led the way into the house. "Grimes has worked himself almost into a fever asking for you."

"Grimes?"

"Yes. Grimes was attacked in our library early this morning by some unknown person, and is in bed with a bad wound on his temple and a tendency to hysteria," McIntyre explained.

"Come upstairs."

Kent handed his cane and hat to the footman and followed Colonel McIntyre, who stalked ahead without another word. As they mounted the stairs Kent glanced at the folded paper which he still held, and was surprised to see that it was a check. The signature showed him that he had unintentionally walked off with Mrs. Brewster's property. His decision to hand it to Colonel McIntyre was checked by the Colonel disappearing inside a bedroom, with a muttered injunction to "wait there," and Kent stuffed the check inside his vest pocket. It would serve as an excuse to interview Mrs. Brewster again before leaving the house. He was determined to have an answer to the question he had put to her in the limousine. Why had she gone to the police court, and why kept her presence there a secret?

When Colonel McIntyre reappeared in the hall he was accompanied by Detective Ferguson. "Sorry to keep you standing, Kent," he said. "I have sent for you and Ferguson, first because Grimes insists on seeing you, and second, because I am determined that this midnight house-breaking shall be thoroughly investigated and put an end to. This way," and he led them into a large airy bedroom on the third floor, to which Grimes had been carried unconscious that morning, instead of to his own bedroom in the servants' quarters.

Grimes, with his head swathed in bandages, was a woe-begone object. He greeted Colonel McIntyre and the detective with a sullen glare, but his eyes brightened at sight of Kent, and he moved a feeble hand in welcome.

"Sit down, sirs," he mumbled. "There's chairs for all."

"Don't worry about us," remarked McIntyre cheerily. "Just tell us how you got that nasty knock on the head."

"I dunno, sir; it came like a clap o' thunder," Grimes tried to lift his head, but gave over the attempt as excruciating pain followed the effort.

"What hour of the morning was it?" asked Ferguson.

"About one o'clock, as near as I can tell, sir."

"And what were you doing in the library at that hour, Grimes?" demanded McIntyre.

"Trying to find out what your household was up to, sir," was Grimes' unexpected answer, and McIntyre started.

"Explain your meaning, Grimes," he commanded sternly.

"You can do it better than I can, sir," retorted Grimes. "You know the reason every one's searching the room with the seven doors."

"The room with the seven doors!" echoed Ferguson. "Which is that?"

"Grimes means the library." McIntyre's tone was short. "I have no idea, Grimes, what your allegations mean. Be more explicit."

The butler eyed him in no friendly fashion. "Wasn't Mr. Turnbull arrested in that very room?" he demanded. "And what was he looking for?"

"Mr. Turnbull's presence has been explained," replied McIntyre. "He came here disguised as a burglar on a wager with my daughter, Miss Barbara."

"Ah, did he now?" Grimes' rising inflection indicated nervous tension. "Did a man with a bad heart come here in the dead of night for nothing but that foolishness?" Grimes glared at his three visitors. "You bet he didn't."

Ferguson, who had followed the dialogue between McIntyre and his servant with deep attention, addressed the excited man.

"Why did Mr. Turnbull enter Colonel McIntyre's library on Monday night disguised as a burglar?" he asked.

Grimes, by a twist of his head, managed to regard the detective out of the corner of his eye.

"Aye, why did he?" he repeated. "That's what I went to the library last night to find out."

"Did you discover anything?" The question shot from McIntyre, and both Ferguson and Kent watched him as they waited for Grimes' reply. The butler took his time.

"No, sir."

McIntyre threw himself back in his chair and his eyebrows rose in interrogation as he touched his forehead significantly and glanced at Grimes. That the butler caught his meaning was evident from his expression, but he said nothing. The detective was the first to speak.

"Did you hear any one break into the house when you were prowling around, Grimes?" he asked.

"No, sir."

The detective turned to Colonel McIntyre. "After finding Grimes did you search the house?" he inquired.

"Yes. The patrolman, O'Ryan, and my new footman, Murray, went with me through the entire house, and we found all doors and windows to the front and rear of the house securely locked," responded McIntyre; "except the window of the reception room on the ground floor. That was closed but unlatched."

Kent wondered if the grimace which twisted the butler's face was meant for a smile.

"That there window was locked when I went to bed," Grimes stated with slow distinctness. "And I was the last person in this house to go to my room."

McIntyre started to speak when Ferguson stopped him.

"Just let me handle this case," he said persuasively. "You have called in the police," and as McIntyre commenced some uncomplimentary remark, he added with sternness. "Don't interfere, sir. Now, Grimes, your statements imply one of two things--some member of the household either went downstairs after you had retired, and opened the window in the reception room to admit the person who afterwards attacked you in the library, or"--Ferguson paused significantly, "some member of this household knocked you senseless in the library. Which was it?"

There was a tense silence. McIntyre, by an obvious effort, refrained from speech as they waited for Grimes' answer.

"I dunno who hit me." Grimes avoided looking at the three men. "But some one did, and that window in the reception room was locked when I went upstairs to my bedroom after every one had retired. I'm telling you God's truth, sir."

McIntyre eyed him in wrathful silence, then turned to his companions.

"The blow has knocked Grimes silly," he commented. "There is certainly no motive for any of us to attack Grimes, nor has any trace of a weapon been found such as must have been used against Grimes. O'Ryan and I looked particularly for it, after removing Grimes from the Venetian casket, where my daughter Helen, Mrs. Brewster and I discovered him lying unconscious."

"What's this Venetian casket like?" asked Ferguson before Kent could question McIntyre.

"It is a fine sample of carving of the Middle Ages," replied McIntyre. "I purchased the pair when in Venice years ago. They are over six feet in length, about three feet wide, and rest on a carved base. There is a door at the end through which it was customary in the Middle Ages to slide the body, after embalming, for the funeral ceremonies, after which the body was removed, placed in another casket and buried. There is a square opening or peep hole on the top of the casket through which you can look at the body; a cleverly concealed door covers this opening. In fact," added McIntyre, "the door at the end is not at first discernible, and is hard to open, unless one has the knack of doing so."

"Hum! It looks as if whoever put Grimes inside the casket was familiar with it," remarked Ferguson dryly, and McIntyre bit his lip. "Guess I'll go and take a look at the casket. I'll come back, Grimes."

Kent rose with the others and started to follow them to the door, but Grimes beckoned him to approach the bed. The butler waited until he heard McIntyre's heavy tread and the lighter footfall of the detective recede down the hall before speaking.

"I was only going to say, sir," he whispered as Kent, at a sign from him, stooped over the bed, "I got a box of aconitine pills for Mrs. Brewster on Sunday--the stuff that poisoned Mr. Turnbull," he paused to explain.

"Yes, go on," urged Kent, catching the man's excitement. "You gave it to Mrs. Brewster--"

"No, sir; I didn't; I left the box on the hall table," Grimes cleared his throat nervously. "I dunno who picked up that box o' poison, Mr. Kent; so help me God, I dunno!"

Kent thought rapidly. "Have you told any one of this?" he asked.

Grimes nodded. "Only one person," he admitted. "I spoke to Miss Barbara last night as she was going to bed." Grimes laid a hot hand on Kent's and glanced fearfully around the room. "Bend nearer, sir; I don't want none other to hear me. Just before I got that knockout blow in the library last night, I heard the swish of skirts--and Miss Barbara was the only living person who knew I knew about the poison."

Kent stared in stupefaction at the butler. He was aroused by a cold voice from the doorway.

"We are waiting for you, Kent," and Colonel McIntyre stood aside to let him pass from the room ahead of him, then without a backward glance at the injured butler, he closed and locked the bedroom door.

CHAPTER XVIII. THE FATAL PERIOD

As Kent walked into the library he found Colonel McIntyre by his side; the latter's even breathing gave no indication of the haste he had made down the staircase to catch up with Kent.

Detective Ferguson hardly noted their arrival, his attention being given wholly to the examination of the Venetian casket which had played such an important part in the drama of the night before. The casket and its companion piece stood on either side of the room near a window recess. The long straight shape of the high boxes on their graceful base gave no indication of the use to which they had been put in ancient days, but made attractive as well as unique pieces of furniture.

Kent crossed the library and, after looking inside the casket, examined the exterior with care.

"Don't touch that crest," cautioned Ferguson, observing that Kent's glance remained focused on the blood-stained, raised letter "B" and the carving back of it. "In fact, don't touch any part of the casket, I'm trying to get finger prints."

Kent barely heard the warning as he turned to McIntyre.

"Haven't I seen that letter 'B' design on your stationery, Colonel?" he asked.

"Barbara uses it," was the reply. "She fancied the antique lettering and copied the 'B' for the engraver; she is handy with her pen, you know."

"Did she wish the 'B' for a seal?" inquired Kent.

"Yes, she had a seal made like it also." McIntyre moved closer to the casket. "Found anything, Ferguson?"

The detective withdrew his head from the opening at the end of the casket, and regarded the furniture vexedly.

"Not a thing," he acknowledged. "Except I am convinced that it required dexterity to slip Grimes inside the casket. The butler is small and slight, but he must have been unconscious from that tap on the forehead and, therefore, a dead weight. Whoever picked him up must have been some athlete, and"--running his eyes up and down Colonel McIntyre's well-knit, erect frame--"pretty familiar with the workings of this casket."

"Pooh! It's not so difficult a feat," McIntyre shrugged his shoulders disdainfully. "My daughters, as children, used to play hide and seek inside the casket with each new governess."

Ferguson stepped forward briskly. "Mr. Kent, let me see if I can lift you inside the casket; make yourself limp--that's it!" as Kent, entering into the investigation heart and soul, relaxed his muscles and fell back against the detective.

A moment later he was swung upward and pushed head-first inside the casket and the door closed. The air, though close, was not unpleasant and Kent, his eyes growing gradually accustomed to the dark interior, tried to discover the trap door at the top of the box but without success. Putting out his hands he felt along the top. The height of the casket did not permit him to sit up, so he was obliged to slide his body down toward his feet to feel along the sides of the casket. This maneuver soon brought his knees in violent contact with the top, and at the sound Ferguson opened the door and assisted him out.

"Had enough of it?" he asked, viewing Kent's reddened cheeks with faint amusement. "I wonder if Grimes could breathe in there for any lengthy period. If so, it would help establish the time which elapsed between his being incarcerated and your finding him, Colonel."

"How so?" demanded McIntyre.

"Well, if he couldn't get air and you hadn't discovered him at once, he'd have died," explained Ferguson. "If you did find him immediately the person who knocked him down must have made a lightning escape."

"Air does get in the casket in some way," broke in Kent. "It wasn't so bad inside. Colonel McIntyre," Kent stopped a moment to remove a piece of red sealing wax clinging to the cuff of his suit. It had not been there when he entered the casket. Kent dropped the wax in his vest pocket as he again addressed his host. "Who first discovered Grimes in the casket?"

"Mrs. Brewster."

"And what was Mrs. Brewster doing in the library at that hour?" glancing keenly at McIntyre as he put the question.

"She could not sleep and came down for a book," explained the Colonel.

Ferguson, who had walked several times around the library, looking behind first one and then the other of the seven doors, paused to ask:

"What attracted Mrs. Brewster's attention to the casket?"

"The blood stain on its side," McIntyre answered.

"What--that!" Ferguson eyed McIntyre incredulously. "Come, sir, do you mean to tell me she noticed that little bit of a stain in a dark room?"

"She had an electric torch," shortly.

"But why should she turn the torch on this casket?" persisted the detective. "She came to the library for a book, and the bookcases are in another part of the room."

"Quite so, but the book she wished was lying on the top of this casket," replied McIntyre, meeting their level looks with one equally steadfast. "I know because I left the book there."

Ferguson glanced from McIntyre to Kent and back again at the Colonel in nonplussed silence. The explanation was pat.

"I'd like to talk with Mrs. Brewster," he remarked dryly.

"Certainly." McIntyre pressed an electric button. The summons was answered immediately by the new servant, Murray. "Ask Mrs. Brewster if she can see Detective Ferguson in the library, Murray," McIntyre directed.

"Beg pardon, sir, but Mrs. Brewster has just gone out," and with a bow Murray withdrew.

Kent, who had drawn forward a chair preparatory to sitting down and participating in the interview with the widow, changed his mind.

"I must leave at once," he said, after consulting his watch. "Please inform Mrs. Brewster, Colonel, that I will be in my office this afternoon, and I expect her to make me the visit she postponed this morning. Ferguson," turning back to address the detective, "you'll find me at the Saratoga for the next hour. Good morning," and paying no attention to Colonel McIntyre's request to remain, he left the room.

There was no one in the hall and Kent debated a moment whether or not to ring for the servant and ask to see Barbara, but, at sight of the hall table, Grimes' confidences recurred to him and drove everything else out of his mind. Stopping before the table he contemplated its smooth surface before moving the few ornaments it held. Satisfied that no pillbox stood behind any of them, he pulled open the two drawers and tumbled their contents about. His efforts only brought to light some half-empty cigarette boxes, matches, a scratch pad or two, and old visiting cards.

Kent shut the drawers, picked up his hat, and took his cane from the tall china umbrella-stand by the hall table. As he stepped through the front doorway he caught sight of the end of his cane, which he was carrying tucked under his arm. Fastened to the ferule of the cane was the round top of a paste-board pill box.

Kent backed so swiftly into the house again that his figure blocked the closing of the front door, which he had started to pull shut after him. Letting the door close gently he walked back to the umbrella stand. It was a tall heavy affair, and he had some difficulty in tipping it over and letting its contents spill on the floor. A soft exclamation escaped him as three little pellets rolled past him, and then came the bottom of a box.

With hasty fingers Kent picked them up, placed them in the box, and fitted on the top, first carefully smoothing over the hole made by his cane when thrust into the umbrella stand by the footman. Replacing the stand he wrapped the box containing the pills in his handkerchief and hurried from the house.

Kent found the operative from Detective Headquarters sitting on duty in Rochester's living room when he entered that apartment a quarter of an hour later.

"Any one called here?" he asked, as the man, whom he had met the night before, greeted him.

"Not a soul, Mr. Kent." Nelson suppressed a yawn; his relief was late in coming, and he had had little sleep the night before. "There's been no disturbance of any kind, not even a ring at the telephone."

Kent considered a moment, then sat down by the telephone and gave a number to Central.

"That you, Sylvester?" he called into the mouth-piece. "If Mrs. Brewster comes to the office, telephone me at Mr. Rochester's apartment, Franklin 52. Don't let

Mrs. Brewster leave until I have seen her."

"Yes, sir," came the reply, and Kent hung up the receiver.

"Had any luncheon?" he asked Nelson as the man loitered around.

"Not yet"--Nelson's eyes brightened at the word. It was long past his usual meal hour.

"Run down to the caf on the first floor and tell the head waiter to give you a square meal and charge it to me," Kent directed. "Order something substantial; you must be used up."

The man hung back. "Thank you, Mr. Kent, but I don't like to leave here until my relief comes," he objected.

"That's all right, I'll stay in the apartment until you return," and Kent settled the question by opening the door leading into the outer corridor. "Ferguson will be around shortly, so hurry."

Kent watched the man scurry toward the elevator shaft, then returned to Rochester's apartment and once more took up the telephone. The operative's reluctance to leave the apartment unguarded had altered his plans somewhat.

"Is this Dr. Stone's office?" he asked a moment later, as a faint "hello," came over the wire. "Oh, doctor, this is Kent. Please come over to Rochester's apartment; I would like to consult you in regard to an important matter. You'll come now? Thanks."

The doctor kept Kent waiting less than five minutes. The clock was striking one when he appeared, bland and smiling. Hardly waiting for him to select a seat Kent flung himself into a chair in front of Rochester's desk and laid the pill box on the writing pad.

"Now, doctor," he began, and his manner gained in seriousness, "what, in your opinion, killed Jimmie Turnbull?"

"The post-mortem examination proved that he had swallowed aconitine in sufficient quantity to cause death," Stone replied. "He undoubtedly died from the effects of that poison."

"Is aconitine difficult to procure?" asked Kent.

"It is often prescribed for fevers." Stone made himself comfortable in a near-by chair. "Aconitine is the alkaloid of aconite. I believe that in India it is frequently employed, not only for the destruction of wild beasts, but for criminal purposes.

The India variety is known as the Bish poison."

Kent started--Bish poison--was he never to get away from the letter "B"?

"Can you procure Bish in this country?" he asked.

Stone considered the question. "You might be able to purchase it from some Hindoo residing or traveling in the United States," he said, after a pause. "I doubt if you could buy it in a drug store."

Kent heaved a sigh of relief as he hitched his chair closer to the physician.

"Did you prescribe a dose of aconitine for Mrs. Brewster recently?" he asked.

"I did, for an attack of rheumatic neuralgia." Stone eyed him curiously. "What then, Kent?"

"Is this the box the medicine came in?" and Kent placed the cover in Stone's hand.

Stone turned the paste-board over and studied the defaced label. "I cannot answer that question positively," he said. "The label bears my name and that of the druggist, but the directions are missing."

"But the number's on it," put in Kent swiftly. "Come, Stone, call up the druggist, repeat the number to him, and ask if it calls for your aconitine prescription."

Stone hesitated as if about to speak, then, reaching out his hand, he picked up the telephone and held a short conversation with the drug clerk of the Thompson Pharmacy.

"That is the box which contained the aconitine pills for Mrs. Brewster," he said, when he had replaced the telephone. "Now, Kent, I have secured the information you wished; kindly tell me your reasons for desiring it."

It was Kent's turn to hesitate. "Do you know many instances where aconitine was used by murderers?" he questioned.

"N-no. I believe it was the drug used in the celebrated Lamson poison case," replied the physician slowly. "I cannot recall any others just at the moment."

"How about suicides?"

"It is seldom, if ever, used for suicides." Stone spoke with more assurance. "I have found in my practice, Kent, that suicides can be classed as follows: drowning by the young, pistols by the adult, and hanging by the aged; women generally prefer asphyxiation, using illuminating gas. But this is beside the question, unless"--bending a penetrating look at his companion--"unless you believe Jimmie Turnbull committed suicide."

"That idea has occurred to me," admitted Kent. "But it doesn't square with other facts which have developed, nor is it in keeping with the character of the man."

"Men who suffer from a mortal disease sometimes commit desperate acts not at all in accord with their previous conduct," responded Stone gravely. "Come, Kent, you have not answered my question. Why did you wish information about this box of aconitine pills prescribed for Mrs. Brewster during her attack of neuralgia?"

"You have just stated that aconitine is not usually administered to murder a person," Kent spoke seriously, choosing his words with care. "Do you wonder then, that I consider it more than a coincidence that Jimmie Turnbull should have died from a dose of that poison, and that the drug should have been prescribed for one of the inmates of the house he visited shortly before his death?"

The physician sat upright, his face had grown gray. "Mr. Kent," he commenced indignantly, "are you aware what you are insinuating? Are you, also, aware that Mrs. Brewster is my cousin, a charming, honorable woman, without a stain on her character?"

Kent set the bottom of the box containing the pills in front of the doctor.

"I have found out that this box, with its dangerous drug, was left on the hall table in the McIntyre house; apparently any one had access to its contents, therefore my remarks are not directed against Mrs. Brewster any more than against any person in the McIntyre household, from the Colonel to the servants. I found these three pills at the McIntyre house this morning; how many did your prescription call for?"

Stone picked up the small pills and, as he balanced them in his palm, his manner grew more alert. Suddenly he dropped two back in the box and touched the third pill with the tip of his tongue; not content with that he crushed it in his fingers, sniffed the drug, and again tested it with his tongue. His expression was peculiar as he looked up at Kent.

"These are not aconitine pills," he stated positively. "They are nitro-glycerine. How did they get in this box?"

Kent rubbed his chin in bewilderment. The box bearing the aconitine label and the pills had all rolled out of the china umbrella stand, and he had taken it for granted that the pills belonged in the box.

"I found them loose in the same receptacle," he explained. "And concluded they were what remained of the aconitine pills which Grimes, the McIntyre butler, said he left on the hall table Sunday afternoon."

Stone smiled with what Kent, who was watching him closely, judged to be an odd mixture of relief and apprehension.

"You could not have found more dissimilar medicine to go in this pill box, although the two kinds of pills are identical in color and size," he said. "Aconitine depresses the heart action while the other stimulates it."

The physician's statement fell on deaf ears. Raising his head after contemplating the pills, Kent had looked across the room and his glance had fallen on a wing chair, standing just inside the doorway of the living room, and thrown partly in shadow by the portieres. The wing of the chair appeared to move. Kent rubbed his eyes and looking again, caught the same slight movement.

Bounding toward the chair Kent saw that the brown shape which he had mistaken for part of the tufted upholstery was the sleek brown hair of a man's well-shaped head. He halted abruptly on meeting the gaze of a pair of mocking eyes.

"Rochester?" he gasped unbelievingly. "Rochester!"

His partner laughed softly as Stone approached. "I have been an interested listener," he said. "Let me complete the good doctor's argument. Nitro-glycerine would have benefitted Jimmie Turnbull and his feeble heart; whereas the missing aconitine pills killed him."

Stone regarded him with severity. "How did you get in this apartment?" he demanded, declining the challenge Rochester had offered in addressing his opinion of Turnbull's death directly to him.

Rochester dangled his bunch of keys in the physician's face and smiled at his excited partner. "If you two hadn't been so absorbed in your conversation you would have heard me walk in," he remarked.

"Where have you been?" demanded Kent, partly recovering from his astonishment which had deprived him of speech.

"I decided to take a vacation at a moment's notice." Rochester spoke with the same slow drawl which was characteristic of him. "You should be accustomed to my eccentricities by this time, Harry."

"We are," announced Detective Ferguson from the hallway, where he and Nelson had been silent witnesses of the scene. "And we'll give you a chance to explain them in the police court."

"On what charge?" demanded Rochester.

"Poisoning your room-mate, Mr. Turnbull," replied the detective, drawing out a pair of handcuffs. "You are mighty clever, Mr. Rochester. I've got to hand it to you for your mysterious disappearances in and out of this apartment, and for murdering Mr. Turnbull right in the police court in the presence of the judge, police officials, and spectators."

Kent stepped forward at sight of the handcuffs and laid a restraining hand on the detective's shoulder. Rochester saw the movement, guessed Kent's intention, and smiled.

"We can settle the case here," he said cheerfully. "No need of troubling the police judge. Now, Mr. Detective, how did I kill Jimmie Turnbull before all those people without any one becoming aware of the fact?"

"Slipped the poison in the glass of water you handed him," answered Ferguson promptly. "A nervy sleight-of-hand, but you'll swing for it."

Rochester's smile was exasperating as he turned to Dr. Stone.

"Judging from Stone's remarks about aconitine--which I overheard," he interpolated. "I gather the doctor is tolerably familiar with the action of the drug. Does aconitine kill instantly, doctor?"

Stone cleared his throat before speaking. "No; the fatal period averages about four hours," he said, and Rochester's eyes sparkled as he looked up at the detective.

"Jimmie died almost immediately after I handed him that drink of water," he declared. "If you wish to know who administered that aconitine poison, you will have to find out who Jimmie was with at the McIntyre house in the early hours of Tuesday morning."

The sharp imperative ring of the telephone bell cut the silence which followed. Kent, standing nearest the instrument, picked it up, and recognized Sylvester's voice over the wire.

"A message has just come, Mr. Kent," he called, "from Mrs. Brewster saying that she will be in your office at four o'clock."

CHAPTER XIX. THE RED SEAL AGAIN

Harry Kent inserted his key in his office door with more vigor than good judgment, and spent some seconds in re-adjusting it in the lock. Once inside the office he put up the latch and closed the door. A glance around the empty office showed him that Sylvester had obeyed his telephone instructions and gone out to luncheon.

Kent noted with satisfaction as he put his hat and cane in the coat closet that he had over two hours before Mrs. Brewster's expected arrival; ample time in which to consider in quietude the events of the past few days, and plan for his interview with the pretty widow. He had spent the time between Rochester's sudden reappearance and a hastily swallowed lunch at a downtown caf, in arranging bail for Rochester. Ferguson had proved obdurate and had persisted in taking the lawyer to Police Headquarters.

Dr. Stone had accompanied the trio, and his testimony, supported by two chemists, regarding the time required for aconitine poison to act, had gone far to weaken the detective's case against Rochester.

Rochester, to Kent's unbounded astonishment, had appeared indifferent to the whole proceedings; and to his partner's urgent inquiries as to where he had spent the past four days, and why he had disappeared, he had returned one invariable answer.

"I'll explain in good time, Harry," and it was not until they were leaving Police Headquarters that his apathy vanished.

"When are you to see Mrs. Brewster?" he asked.

"She will be at our office at four o'clock. Say, Phil"--but Rochester, shaking off his detaining hand, darted across the street and sprang into a passing taxi bearing the sign, "For Hire," and that was the last Kent had seen of his elusive partner.

Kent dropped into his chair and glanced askance at the mail piled in neat array on his desk; he was not in a frame of mind to handle routine office business. Other clients would have to wait until later in the day. A memorandum pad, bearing a message in Sylvester's precise penmanship attracted his wandering attention and he picked it up.

"Mr. Kent:" he read. "Colonel McIntyre called just after I talked with you on the 'phone; he waited in your office for half an hour, then left, stating he would come back. Miss Barbara McIntyre called immediately afterwards, but would not wait more than five minutes. Mr. Clymer came as she was going out and left a note on your desk. I will return soon.

"SYLVESTER."

Kent laid down the pad and picked up a twisted three-cornered note bearing his name in pencil. Unfolding it, he scanned the hurriedly written lines:

"Dear Kent--McIntyre telephoned there were new developments in the Turnbull affair. Will be back later.

"Yours--

"B. A. CLYMER."

Kent judged from the use of his initials that Clymer was stirred out of his ordinary calm, nothing else explained his failure to sign his full name, and he wondered what confidences McIntyre had made to the bank president.

Tossing down the note, Kent lighted his pipe, tilted back in his swivel chair, and reviewed the facts which implicated Rochester in Jimmie Turnbull's murder. Rochester's quarrels with Jimmie, his persistent assertion that his friend had died from angina pectoris, his unexplained disappearance on Tuesday night, the fake telegram from Cleveland stating he was there, the withdrawal of his bank deposits, the forged checks, his mysterious visits to his own apartment, when considered together, presented a chain of circumstantial evidence connecting him with the crime. But in the light of Dr. Stone's testimony, the poison "could not have been administered in the glass of water Rochester had given Jimmie in the police court."

Four hours at least had to elapse before the fatal dose of aconitine could take effect--four hours! Kent told them off on his fingers; it placed the crime in the McIntyre house. Which one of its inmates administered the poison to Jimmie and how had it been done? What motive had prompted the cashier's murder?

It was preposterous to think that either of the twins was guilty of the crime. Helen's devotion to Jimmie, her insistence upon an autopsy being held indicated her innocence. She had stated at the inquest that she had not known the burglar's identity; Kent paused as the thought occurred to him--the twins had swapped identities on the witness stand, and therefore Helen had not been called upon to answer that question! To the best of his recollection she had only been asked if she had recognized Jimmie in the court room and not at her home. But Helen it was who had summoned Officer O'Ryan on discovering the burglar and had him arrested. She surely would never have done so had she guessed his identity.

As for Barbara McIntyre--Kent's heart beat faster at thought of the girl he loved so well. Circumstantial evidence had seemed for a time to involve her in the crime. Grimes' outrageous insinuation that he had been assaulted on account of confiding to her that the box of aconitine pills had been left on the hall table where any one could get them, was the outcome of his battered condition. When physical strength returned, the butler would forget his hallucinations. The handkerchief with its embroidered letter "B," used by Jimmie to inhale the fumes from his amyl nitrite capsules, was finally traced to its rightful owner--Mrs. Brewster.

And Mrs. Brewster was due in his office within a very short time. Kent's square jaw became more pronounced; she should not leave until she had either confessed her connection with Turnbull's death, or established her innocence. Surely it would be easy for Mrs. Brewster to do so, but--aconitine had been prescribed for her; she was familiar with the poison, she had it at hand, she went to the police court, and kept her trip a secret, and she had laughed when Jimmie was carried dying from the court room. But what motive could have inspired her to murder Jimmie? Was he an old lover--Kent, unable to keep quiet any longer, rose and paced up and down the office, stopping a moment to glance out of the window. As he passed the safe he saw the door was ajar. Kent paused abruptly. Who had opened the safe?

Crossing to the outer office he looked around; no one was there. It flashed into Kent's mind that he had seen Rochester's light top coat and walking stick in the coat closet as he hung up his hat on his arrival, and he again opened the closet door. The coat and stick were still there; so Rochester had come to the office immediately after leaving him, and carelessly left the safe open! Kent smiled in spite of his vexation; the act was typical of his eccentric partner.

Going back to his own office Kent opened the safe and glanced inside. The pigeon holes and compartments appeared untouched, except the door of one small compartment on Rochester's side. An envelope was wedged in such a manner that the small door would not shut and that had prevented the closing of the outer safe door.

Kent, preparatory to shutting the safe, drew out the envelope intending to place it in another pigeon-hole where there was more room. As he turned the envelope over he was thunderstruck to recognize it as the one which Helen McIntyre had placed in the safe on Wednesday morning. He had last seen the envelope lying on the table in the smoking porch of the Club de Vingt, from whence it had mysteriously disappeared, and now it was back again in Rochester's safe!

Had it ever been missing from the safe? The question forced itself on Kent as he returned to his chair, envelope in hand, and sat down before his desk. He had accepted Detective Ferguson's statement that he had removed the envelope from the safe, and therefore had never looked in the compartment where Helen had put it to verify its disappearance.

Ferguson had removed it, Kent concluded as he examined the envelope with more care; it was the identical one, unaddressed, with the same red seal holding down the flap. The same red seal, but with a difference--a corner was missing.

Kent stared at the seal for a moment in doubt, then his fingers sought his vest pocket and fumbled about for a minute. Taking out Mrs. Brewster's check, he laid it on the desk alongside the envelope, unfolded it, and picked out a piece of red sealing wax which had slid inside the check. Kent placed the red wax on the broken section of the seal--it fitted exactly, forming a perfect letter "B."

Kent sat in dumbfounded silence, regarding the red seal and the envelope. The piece of wax broken off from the seal had caught on his coat sleeve when he had been in the Venetian casket in the library at the McIntyre house. It was proof positive that not only he had been in the casket, but the sealed envelope also. Helen McIntyre had left the envelope in his care. Mrs. Brewster and Colonel McIntyre had both been present when the envelope was stolen from him. Which of them had taken it? Which one had afterwards secreted it in the Venetian casket? And which had brought it back to the safe in his office?

Colonel McIntyre had been in his office within the hour--the question was answered, and Kent's eyes brightened, then clouded--Barbara had been there as well, and Grimes had stated that before he received a knock-out blow in the McIntyre library he heard the swish of skirts!

Kent laid his hand on the envelope. It was time that he found out what it contained; but his finger, inserted under the flap, paused as his eyes fell on the check bearing Mrs. Brewster's signature. It was the check he had picked up from the floor of the McIntyre limousine that morning and inadvertently carried away with him.

From her signature his glance wandered to Sylvester's memorandum pad; it was uncanny the way his eye picked out the letter "B" as he stared at Clymer's note and its signature. Slowly his hand dropped away from the envelope and he left it lying forgotten on the desk as he picked up piece after piece of blotting paper, glancing intently at each and finally, pulling open a drawer of his desk, he hunted in feverish haste for a hand-mirror.

Some ten minutes later Kent rose, placed the papers he had been examining in the inside pocket of his coat and, using the private entrance from his office into the corridor, he hurried away.

When Helen McIntyre entered the office of Rochester and Kent for the second time that afternoon she found Sylvester transcribing stenographic notes on his typewriter.

"Mr. Kent is expecting you, miss," he said, holding open the inner office door, and with a courteous word of thanks, Helen passed the clerk and the door closed behind her. Kent rose at her approach and bowed formally.

"Take this chair," he suggested, and not until she was seated did Helen realize he had placed her where the light fell full upon her. "I asked you to come here," he began, as she waited for him to speak, "Because I must have your confidence--if I am to aid you. Did you meet, recognize, and talk to Jimmie Turnbull in your house sometime between Monday midnight and his arrest on Tuesday morning?"

She colored hotly, then paled. "My testimony at the inquest,"--she commenced, but he gave her no opportunity to add more.

"Your testimony there does not cover the question," he explained. "You stated then that you had not recognized Jimmie in the court room. Had you already penetrated his disguise at your house?"

"And if I had?"

"Did you?" Kent was doggedly persistent, and Helen's fingers closed around her handbag with convulsive force. Why had she not sent Barbara to see Kent in her place?

"Did I what?" she parried.

"Did you recognize and talk with Jimmie Turnbull in your house?"

"I talked with him, yes," she admitted, and her voice dropped almost to a whisper.

"As Jimmie Turnbull or Smith the burglar?"

"As Jimmie"--she confessed, after a slight pause.

"Then why did you go through the farce of having Jimmie arrested as a burglar?" Kent demanded.

"So that Barbara might win her wager," promptly. Kent stared at her incredulously.

"Do you mean that, notwithstanding the risk to which you were subjecting him with his weak heart, you kept up the farce simply that Barbara might win an idiotic wager?" Kent asked.

Helen passed one nervous hand over the other; her palms were hot and dry, and two hectic spots had appeared in each white cheek.

"Jimmie was quite well Monday night," she protested. "He--he--had some heart medicine with him."

"Amyl nitrite?"

"No."

"Nitro-glycerine?"

"I--I think that was it, I am not quite sure," she spoke with uncertainty, and Kent knew that she lied. His heart sank.

"Did he swallow any medicine in your presence?"

She shook her head vigorously. "No, he did not."

Kent lowered his voice. "Did you see him take Mrs. Brewster's aconitine pills off the hall table?"

Helen shifted her gaze to his face and then back to her ever restless hands. "No," she said. "I did not see him take the pills."

Kent studied her in a silence which, to her, seemed never-ending.

"I want the true answer to this question," he announced with meaning emphasis. "Why did Jimmie go in disguise to your house on Monday night?"

Helen blanched. "How should I know," she muttered evasively. "He--he didn't come to see me--the admission was barely above a whisper.

"But you know what transpired in your house on Monday night?" demanded Kent eagerly.

His question met with no response, and he repeated it, but still the girl remained silent. Kent gave her a moment's grace, then drawing out the unaddressed envelope from his pocket he held it toward her. A low cry broke from her, and her expression changed as she caught sight of the broken seal.

"You have opened it!"

"Not yet," Kent held the envelope just beyond her reach. "I will only give it to you with the understanding that you open the envelope now in my presence and let me see its contents."

Helen drew back, then impulsively extended her hand.

"I agree," she said. "Give me the envelope."

"Stop!" The word rang out, startling Kent as well as Helen, and Mrs. Brewster, whose noiseless entrance a few seconds before had gone unobserved, hurried to them. "The envelope is mine."

CHAPTER XX. THE UNKNOWN EQUATION

"No, no," protested Helen vehemently. "You shall not give the envelope to Margaret--you must not."

"It is mine," insisted the widow with equal vehemence.

"Mrs. Brewster." Kent withheld the envelope from both women. "Will you tell me the contents of this envelope?"

"No," curtly. "It is not your affair."

"It is my affair," retorted Kent with equally shortness of manner. "I insist on an answer to my questions in the limousine this morning. How came your handkerchief in Jimmie's possession, and why did you go to the police court and, yet keep your presence there a secret?"

"Jimmie must have picked up the handkerchief when in the McIntyre house," she answered sullenly. "I presume he forgot to provide him self with one in his make-up as burglar. As regards your second question I admit I did go to the police court out of curiosity--I wanted to find out what was going on. You," with a resentful glance at Helen, "treated me as an outsider, and I was determined to find out for myself how the burglar farce would end."

"Ah, you term it a farce--is that why you laughed in court?" asked Kent quickly.

Mrs. Brewster changed color. "I feel badly about that," she stammered. "I meant no disrespect to Jimmie, but I have a nervous inclination to laugh--almost hysteria--when excited and overwrought."

"I see," answered Kent slowly. He was distinctly puzzled; Mrs. Brewster's air of candor disarmed suspicion, but--"You saw and talked with Jimmie Turnbull on Monday night?"

"I did not." Her denial was firm.

"Then how did you learn of his arrest?" asked Kent swiftly.

"I overheard him conversing--"

"With whom?" Kent demanded eagerly as she paused as if to reconsider her confidences. Helen, one hand on the desk and the other on the arm of her chair, tried to rise, but her strength had deserted her. "With whom?" repeated Kent as the widow remained silent.

"Jimmie was talking with Grimes," Mrs. Brewster stated slowly. "From what I overheard, he paid Grimes to let him inside the house."

Kent looked perplexed as he gazed first at the widow and then at Helen, who had sunk back in her chair.

"Mrs. Brewster," he began after a pause. "Who gave Jimmie your aconitine pills which Grimes left on the hall table?"

"The murderer."

"Yes, of course." Kent was watching her closely and he detected the tiny beads of perspiration which were gathering on her upper lip. "And who, in your opinion, was the murderer?"

Mrs. Brewster's expression changed--she looked hunted, and her eyes fell before Kent's; abruptly she turned her back on him, to find Colonel McIntyre at her elbow and Barbara just entering the room. Her eyes traveled past the girl until they rested on Philip Rochester and Detective Ferguson hovering behind him. Her face altered.

"I saw Philip Rochester," pointing dramatically toward him, "crawl out of the reception room window and dart into the street just as O'Ryan came in the front door with Helen."

Detective Ferguson could not restrain a joyful exclamation. "So that was it!" he cried. "You were at the McIntyre house, and gave the poison to Turnbull there-- and not in the court room--four hours before he died. You'll swing for that crime, my buck, in spite of your glib tongue and slippery ways."

As he ceased speaking Ferguson's ever ready handcuffs swung suggestively from his hand, but Helen's agonized cry checked his approach toward Rochester, who stood stolidly waiting for him.

"Father! You cannot permit this monstrous injustice, Philip shall not suffer for another. No, Barbara," as her sister strove to quiet her, "we must tell the truth."

"Suppose I tell it for Colonel McIntyre," Rochester advanced as the door opened and Sylvester ushered in Benjamin Clymer. "You have come in time, Clymer," his voice deepened, the voice of a man accustomed to present a case and sway a court. "Wait, Sylvester, sit at that table and take down these charges--"

"Charges?" questioned Kent, watching his partner narrowly; he tossed a steno-graphic pad to Sylvester and made a place for him at his desk. "Go on, Rochester; charges against whom?"

"Charges against the man who, occupying a position of trust, planned to swin-dle the Metropolis Trust Company through forged notes and checks," Rochester stated with slow emphasis. "Jimmie Turnbull learned that you, Clymer, were to visit Colonel McIntyre on Monday night, and he went there in disguise to find out if his suspicions were correct. The investigation cost him his life."

Clymer, who had followed Rochester's statement, first with bewilderment and then with rising wrath, found his voice.

"You drunken scoundrel!" he roared. "How dare you!"

"Dare!" Rochester laughed recklessly. "Jimmie kept his wits to the last; his mind was clear; he recognized you in the prisoner's pen and he tried to call you, but his palsied tongue could not say Ben, but stuttered--B--b--b."

"And what did he wish to tell me?" gasped Clymer, down whose colorless face perspiration trickled.

"Aye, what?" broke in Kent significantly.

"Jimmie may not have gotten the information he wished at your house, Colo-nel McIntyre, but his presence there on Monday night showed the forger he was in danger, and like the human snake he is, he poisoned without warning. Don't move--Sylvester!"

With a backward spring Kent caught his clerk as he sped for the door.

"Don't make any mistake in putting on the handcuffs this time, Ferguson," he shouted. "A forger and a contortionist make a bad customer to reckon with."

CHAPTER XXI. THE RIDDLE ANSWERED

There was absolute stillness in the room; then a babble of exclamations broke out as Sylvester, his expression of dumb surprise giving place to one of fury, struggled to free himself from the detective's firm grip.

"You cannot escape, Sylvester," declared Kent, observing his efforts. "Your carelessness in using your peculiar gift of penmanship in copying Barbara McIntyre's signature in this memorandum of her visit here"--Kent held up a sheet torn from his pad, "gave me the first clew. These, the second," he showed several pieces of blotting paper freshly used. "See, in the mirror here is reflected the impression from your clever imitations of the handwritings of Barbara, Colonel McIntyre, and Mrs. Brewster."

They crowded about Kent, all but Ferguson and his prisoner, who had subsided in his chair with what the detective concluded was dangerous quietude.

"My next step, now that suspicion was directed against Sylvester, was to make personal inquiries regarding him," went on Kent. "Judge Hildebrand, who had just returned to Washington, said that he first met Sylvester at a circus sideshow where he gave exhibitions as a contortionist. One of his special stunts was to slip out of handcuffs and ropes."

"So that explains last night," Ferguson grinned. "You'll not do it again, Sylvester," and he shook an admonitory finger at the erstwhile clerk.

"Judge Hildebrand became interested in Sylvester, found he was handy with his pen and tired of the show business, and gave him an opening by engaging him as confidential clerk," continued Kent. "You will recall, Colonel McIntyre, that you sent business papers in your handwriting and that of your daughters to Judge Hildebrand's office to be typed by his staff. That is how Sylvester became so well acquainted with your writing and was able to forge a letter to the bank treasurer directing him to turn over your negotiable securities to Jimmie Turnbull."

"But how in the world did Sylvester induce Jimmie to present the forged letter?" asked Colonel McIntyre.

Kent turned to the sullen prisoner. "Answer that question, Sylvester," he commanded, and the man roused himself from his dejected attitude.

"Anything in it for me if I do?" he asked with a cunning leer.

"That's for the courts to decide," declared Kent.

The man thought a minute. "I'll take a chance," he said finally. "But that I waited for an opportunity to get my swag out of this safe, I wouldn't have been caught--curse you!" and he scowled at Kent.

"Cut that out," admonished Ferguson with a none too gentle dig in the ribs, and Sylvester continued his statement.

"I overheard Colonel McIntyre tell Judge Hildebrand about his securities and their present value, and the next day he came to consult the judge about engaging a secretary. I fixed up credentials and went to Mr. Turnbull; he believed my story that I was the colonel's new secretary and got the securities." Sylvester paused. "If I'd rested content with that success I'd been all right," he added. "But I was in too great a hurry and forged Mr. Clymer's signature to a check for five thousand dollars and presented it at the Metropolis Trust Company. As luck would have it Mr. Turnbull cashed it for me himself."

"But didn't he suspect you?" exclaimed Clymer. He had gradually recovered from the shock of Rochester's charges on his arrival, and was listening with keen attention to Sylvester's confession.

"No. I made the check payable to Colonel McIntyre and forged his endorsement," Sylvester spoke with an air of pride, and he smiled in malicious enjoyment as, catching his eye, Barbara shrank back and sheltered herself behind Kent. "Mr. Turnbull accepted the check; later something must have aroused his suspicions, and I found when he questioned me that he believed Colonel McIntyre had forged the check."

"Good heavens! You let him think that?" gasped McIntyre; then wrath gained the mastery. "You scoundrel!"

"Oh, I encouraged him to think it," Sylvester grinned again. "You must have handed Mr. Turnbull a raw deal; he was so ready to think evil of you."

"That is a lie!" exclaimed Helen hotly. "When I went downstairs to investigate the noise I heard in the library, father, Jimmie told me who he was to quiet my fright. He showed me a letter, which he had just found on your desk in the library, confessing that you had forged Mr. Clymer's name on the check, and begging Jimmie to conceal your crime and save Barbara and me from the shame of having you exposed as a forger and a thief."

"I never wrote such a letter!" shouted McIntyre, deeply incensed.

"No, it was a clever plan," acknowledged Sylvester. "On one of my trips to your house, Colonel McIntyre, I secured wax impressions of your front door lock. I went to your house Monday night and put the letter among your papers just before Turnbull was admitted by your fool of a butler."

"And you gave Jimmie Turnbull a dose of poison--charged Kent, but Sylvester, his lips gone dry, raised his manacled hands in protest.

"I did not poison him," he cried. "I waited just to see if Turnbull got the letter and to find out what he'd do with the securities, which he had refused to turn over to me. After he had read the forged letter Mr. Turnbull acted sort of faint and went out in the hall. I could just see him put down a box on the hall table and lean against the wall. Then he went into the dining room and came back a second later carrying a glass of water, and I saw him take up and open a small box and toss some white pills into his mouth; then he took a good drink, and, picking up a handkerchief lying on the table, he went back into the library."

There was silence as Sylvester's callous recital of the tragedy ended. Helen, her eyes tearless and dark with suffering, sank slowly back in her chair and rested her head against Barbara's sympathetic shoulder.

"So Turnbull's death was accidental after all," exclaimed Ferguson. "Or was it suicide?"

"Accident," answered Kent. "I found some nitro-glycerine pills in the umbrella stand by the hall table." Colonel McIntyre nodded. "Evidently Turnbull put down his pill box before getting a glass of water, and in his attack of giddiness accidentally opened your box of aconitine pills, Mrs. Brewster, instead of his own, and swallowed a fatal dose, thinking they were nitroglycerine."

Mrs. Brewster bowed her head in agreement. "That must have been it," she said. "However, I saw Colonel McIntyre tear off the paper wrapping and open my package of pills just before dinner, and when I heard that Jimmie had died from aconitine I--I--" she stammered and stopped short.

"You suspected I had murdered him?" asked McIntyre softly.

"Yes," she looked appealingly at him. "Forgive me, I should never have suspected you, but the pills, box and all, were missing the next morning from the hall table."

"Turnbull must have thrown the box into the umbrella stand," explained Kent. "That was where I found it. Did you get the securities, Sylvester?" turning to the prisoner.

"No," sullenly. "She did," and a jerk of his thumb indicated Helen McIntyre.

Helen raised her head and addressed them slowly.

"Jimmie and I expected Barbara to come in at any moment, and he started to leave when we saw you coming downstairs," she turned to Mrs. Brewster. "Jimmie declared that if we were found together I might be compromised. He couldn't explain his presence without exposing father--we both thought you a forger, father," she interpolated, as McIntyre took her hand and pressed it understandingly. "So he insisted that I should treat him like an ordinary burglar--we had both forgotten Barbara's silly wager in our horror about father. Jimmie didn't dare take the securities and father's confession with him for fear he'd be searched at the police station, and the scandal would have come out then."

"True," agreed McIntyre. "Go on, Helen."

"So Jimmie thrust the securities and father's confession into an envelope and sealed it with red wax, using Barbara's seal," explained Helen. "He hadn't time to write an address or message on it, but he told me to return the envelope to him later in the day or give it to Philip Rochester and ask his aid. I brought it here on Wednesday morning and with Harry's permission put the envelope in the safe."

"I tried to get it from there," volunteered Sylvester, "for I overheard Turnbull's plan, before I left by the reception room window."

"So it was you and not Mr. Rochester whom I saw steal out of the window," exclaimed Mrs. Brewster.

"It's not the first time I've been mistaken for him," exclaimed Sylvester calmly.

Kent started and, gazing at Rochester and the clerk, saw there was a general resemblance in coloring and physique.

"Did you present the checks to McDonald at the Metropolis Trust Company bearing Rochester's and my forged signatures?" he asked.

"I did," acknowledged Sylvester. "Mr. Rochester's wardrobe came in very handy for deceiving the casual glance. You know, 'clothes make the man, and want of it the fellow.'"

Kent looked up quickly, struck by an idea.

"Sylvester, did you steal the envelope containing the securities from me at the Club de Vingt?" he asked.

Sylvester shook his head. "No, but she did," pointing to Mrs. Brewster. "It's no lie," as McIntyre uttered an indignant denial. "When Ferguson left here carrying off the securities from under my nose almost--I had spent the whole day trying to learn the safe's combination; I trailed him to the Club de Vingt, and heard the head waiter tell him you, Mr. Kent, were sitting in the small smoking porch, so I climbed up the trumpet vine; oh, it was strong and no climb for one who has done the feats I have in the circus. I reached the porch just in time to see Mrs. Brewster drop her fan, and when the men bent to pick it up she 'lifted' the envelope and concealed it under her scarf."

"Don't," Mrs. Brewster laid a detaining hand on McIntyre as he stepped forward. "The man is telling the truth. I thought it was the envelope you gave me earlier in the evening--it was unaddressed and the red seal was the same."

"Just a moment," interrupted Kent. "What did you do with the envelope?"

"When I returned home I dropped it inside one of the Venetian caskets," Mrs. Brewster replied. "No one ever went near them, and I thought it would be safe there. You see, I was puzzled to know how it had disappeared from the desk in the reception room, where I had left it in one of the pigeon holes, intending to take it later to my room."

"I took the envelope--your envelope--out of the desk," confessed McIntyre. "I would have spoken of it, Margaret, but was hurt that you had left our marriage certificate lying around so carelessly."

"Your what?" Barbara sprang up, astounded.

"Our marriage certificate," repeated McIntyre firmly. "Margaret and I were married last week in Baltimore. We would have told you, Helen, but your peculiar conduct and Barbara's, so angered me that I forbade Margaret to take you into our confidence."

"Father!" Barbara got no further, for Helen had risen. She spoke with quiet dignity.

"You forget, father, that since Monday night we have thought you a forger and, worse, a murderer," her voice faltered. "In our effort to guard you we have become estranged. Margaret"--she held out her hand with an affectionate gesture and with a sob her step-mother kissed her.

"How did this envelope get back inside our safe?" asked Kent a moment later, picking it up and displaying the red seal, intact save for the broken corner.

"I went downstairs about midnight or a little later and into the library," confessed Helen. "What was my surprise and terror to see Grimes holding the envelope. To me it meant father's exposure as a forger. I had a revolver in my hand and struck before I thought. Then I must temporarily have lost my reason. It was only my thought to save father that lent me courage and strength to thrust Grimes inside the casket where Babs and I used to hide. I then returned to my room, and was just coming downstairs again after secreting the envelope, to release Grimes and get medical assistance if need be, when Margaret's screams aroused the household."

McIntyre interrupted his daughter with a hasty gesture, and addressed his wife. "When Detective Ferguson questioned me as to your reason for being in the library, Margaret, I stated you had gone down to get a book left lying on the Venetian casket," he said. "I waited for you to volunteer an explanation of your presence there, but you never made any."

"I went down to get our marriage certificate." Margaret forgot the presence of others and spoke only to him, the love-light in her eyes pleading against the censure she dreaded, as she made her brief confession. "Mr. Clymer sent me a note, inclosing a canceled check, stating the bank officials had decided my signature was a forgery. The check was drawn to Barbara, and on examining it I noticed the peculiar formation of the letter 'B'; it is characteristic of your handwriting and Helen's." She paused, and added:

"I was at a loss what to think. I knew you and Helen wrote alike; Helen's extraordinary behavior to me led me to believe that perhaps she had been short of funds, and forged my name to a check in desperation. Then I remembered seeing you, Charles, open the box containing my aconitine pills, the box's disappearance, and Jimmie's death from that poison"--she raised her hands in an expressive gesture. "Although my reason told me that you might be guilty, my loyalty and love refuted the accusation."

"Margaret!" McIntyre's voice shook with emotion; then controlling himself he turned to Sylvester. "I presume this check was some more of your deviltry?"

Helen answered for the clerk. Removing a soiled paper from her bag she laid it on Kent's desk. "This note was handed to me by Grimes," she explained. "It reads: 'Helen, please cash this check and give money to Mrs. Brewster's dressmaker. Father.' I followed the instructions."

"And gave the money to my sister," Sylvester chuckled at their surprise. "My sister was taught in a French convent, and she is an excellent seamstress, when she isn't drunk, as Mrs. McIntyre knows."

"See here, Sylvester," Clymer broke his long silence. "You were in the police court on a charge of assault and battery brought by your wife on Tuesday morning, and you were in the prisoner's cage at the moment Turnbull died. How then was it possible for you to be at the McIntyre's at midnight on Monday?"

"I was out on bail and appeared in the courtroom just in time for my trial," Sylvester explained. "I did not have to sit in the cage, but recognizing Turnbull I went there to be with him."

Kent placed the forged check bearing Margaret Brewster's signature on the desk. "I take it this check is your work, Sylvester," he said. "You reaped the benefit by having the money paid to your sister. Did you also have the fake telegram delivered to me stating Mr. Rochester was in Cleveland?"

"I faked that," broke in Rochester, before the clerk could make a disclaimer. "I thought it best to disappear for a few days down in Virginia, where I could think things over in peace."

"So it was you, Sylvester, and not Mr. Rochester whom I encountered in his apartment," exclaimed Kent. "How did you get in the apartment?"

"From the fire-escape and along the window ledge to the bathroom window." Sylvester hitched his shoulders. "It was nothing for a man of my agility."

Ferguson eyed him with doubtful respect.

"You have courage," he admitted grudgingly. "Come, we must get to Headquarters," and he aided Sylvester to his feet, but once standing, Sylvester refused to move. Instead he turned to Helen.

"What was that you passed to Mr. Rochester in the police court and he later gave to Mr. Turnbull?" he asked. "Oh, don't deny it, I saw you palm a note, Mr. Rochester, from the young lady."

"There is nothing now to conceal," declared Helen. "After O'Ryan and Jimmie left the house for the police station I grew fearful that Jimmie might over-tax his strength in carrying out the farce of his arrest. So as soon as I could I telephoned to Philip to meet me at the police court and to bring some amyl nitrite capsules with him."

"And the note, Sylvester, which you saw Miss McIntyre give me in court," concluded Rochester, as Helen paused, "told me to hand the capsules to the burglar and to defend him in court. I did both, although badly puzzled by the request." Rochester hesitated. "I carried out your wishes, Helen, without question; but when the burglar's identity was revealed, I jumped to the conclusion that you had used me as an instrument to kill him, for I knew something of the effects of amyl nitrite."

"Great Heavens!" exclaimed Helen, aghast.

Rochester looked at her and bit his lip; he knew of her affection for Jimmie and her attachment to his memory, but he could not kill the hope that when Time had healed the loss, his devotion might some day win her for his own.

"I did you great injustice," he admitted humbly. "But I was fearfully shocked by the scene. I strove to divert suspicion by insisting that Jimmie died from angina pectoris, and then you came, Helen, and demanded an autopsy."

"I had to," Helen broke in. "I could not believe that Jimmie's death was due to natural causes," her voice quivered. "He had been so loyal--so faithful--I could not be less true to him, even if, as I feared, my own dear father was guilty of the crime."

Kent turned and faced Sylvester, who had made a few shuffling steps toward the door.

"You have done incalculable harm by your criminal acts," he said sternly. "But for your lying and trickery Jimmie Turnbull would be alive to-day. I trust the Court will give you the maximum sentence."

Sylvester eyed him insolently. "I've had a run for my money, and I stood to win large sums if things had only gone right," he announced; then addressed Helen directly. "What did you do with the securities?"

"I put the envelope back in the open safe when I was here early this afternoon," she explained.

An oath ripped from Sylvester. "I mistook you for your sister," he snarled. "Had I known it was you, I'd have wrung the securities from you."

Helen stared at his suddenly contorted face. "Ah, you are the man who looked in at the window of the reception room yesterday morning when I was talking to Mr. Kent," she cried. "I recognize you now."

He continued to glare at her. "I also sent you a note by your sister outside the Caf St. Marks to secrete the letter 'B'," his voice rose almost into a shout in his ungovernable rage. "I heard Turnbull tell you to take the envelope to Rochester, and I banked on your bringing it here or to his apartment. D-mn you! You've thwarted me at every turn."

Rochester's powerful hand was clapped across his mouth with such force that the clerk staggered against Ferguson.

"Here you, out you go." The detective shoved the struggling man toward the door leading into the corridor and Clymer sprang to his assistance; a second later Rochester closed the door on their receding figures and found Helen standing by his elbow.

"I must go," she said, turning back to look at her father and his bride.

"Wait a minute." Kent held up an envelope with its fateful red seal. "This was delivered empty at Rochester's apartment last night--it is addressed to him. Who wrote it?"

"I did," exclaimed Mrs. McIntyre. "I felt I must consult either you, Mr. Kent, or Mr. Rochester, so I sent the note to his apartment, but the messenger boy hurried me, and it was not until hours later that I found the note lying on the desk in the reception room and realized I had sent an empty envelope."

"I see." Kent held up another envelope, the red seal broken at the corner. "This is yours, Helen."

Helen hesitated perceptibly before taking the envelope and tearing it open. She handed the securities to her father.

"Here is father's forged confession," she said as she took the remaining paper from the envelope.

"It is a marvelous imitation of my handwriting," declared McIntyre, looking at it carefully, then tearing it into tiny bits he flung them into the scrap-basket and pocketed the securities.

"And to think that I aided Sylvester's plot to gain the securities by engaging him as our clerk," groaned Rochester.

"It was clever of him to seek employment here," agreed Kent. "But like many crooks he over-reached himself through over-confidence. Must you go, Colonel McIntyre?"

"Yes." McIntyre walked over to Helen.

"My dear little girl," he began and his voice was husky with feeling. "How can I show my appreciation of your loyalty to me?"

"By being kind to Harry and Barbara." Helen smiled bravely, although her lips were trembling and for a moment she could not trust herself to speak. "My romance is over; Barbara's is just beginning. And, father, will you and Margaret come home with me--I am so lonely;" then turning blindly away she fairly ran out of the office.

"Go with her," said Rochester, a trifle unsteadily. "It has been a terrible ordeal; God help her to forget!" His voice failed and he swept his hand across his eyes as he held open the door into the corridor and followed McIntyre and his wife outside.

Kent turned impulsively to Barbara, and his arms closed around her as she raised her eyes to meet his, for she knew that the promise they spoke would be loyally fulfilled, and that her haven of love and happiness was reached at last.

www.bookjungle.com *email: sales@bookjungle.com fax: 630-214-0564 mail: Book Jungle PO Box 2226 Champaign, IL 61825*

The Codes Of Hammurabi And Moses
W. W. Davies

QTY

The discovery of the Hammurabi Code is one of the greatest achievements of archaeology, and is of paramount interest, not only to the student of the Bible, but also to all those interested in ancient history...

Religion   **ISBN:** *1-59462-338-4*   **Pages:132**
MSRP $12.95

The Theory of Moral Sentiments
Adam Smith

QTY

This work from 1749. contains original theories of conscience amd moral judgment and it is the foundation for systemof morals.

Philosophy   ISBN: *1-59462-777-0*   **Pages:536**
MSRP $19.95

Jessica's First Prayer
Hesba Stretton

QTY

In a screened and secluded corner of one of the many railway-bridges which span the streets of London there could be seen a few years ago from five o'clock every morning until half past eight, a tidily set-out coffee-stall, consisting of a trestle and board, upon which stood two large tin cans, with a small fire of charcoal burning under each so as to keep the coffee boiling during the early hours of the morning when the work-people were thronging into the city on their way to their daily toil...

Childrens   ISBN: *1-59462-373-2*   **Pages:84**
MSRP $9.95

My Life and Work
Henry Ford

QTY

Henry Ford revolutionized the world with his implementation of mass production for the Model T automobile. Gain valuable business insight into his life and work with his own auto-biography... "We have only started on our development of our country we have not as yet, with all our talk of wonderful progress, done more than scratch the surface. The progress has been wonderful enough but..."

Biographies'   ISBN: *1-59462-198-5*   **Pages:300**
MSRP $21.95

The Art of Cross-Examination
Francis Wellman

QTY

I presume it is the experience of every author, after his first book is published upon an important subject, to be almost overwhelmed with a wealth of ideas and illustrations which could readily have been included in his book, and which to his own mind, at least, seem to make a second edition inevitable. Such certainly was the case with me; and when the first edition had reached its sixth impression in five months, I rejoiced to learn that it seemed to my publishers that the book had met with a sufficiently favorable reception to justify a second and considerably enlarged edition. ..

Pages:412

Reference   **ISBN:** *1-59462-647-2*   *MSRP $19.95*

On the Duty of Civil Disobedience
Henry David Thoreau

QTY

Thoreau wrote his famous essay, On the Duty of Civil Disobedience, as a protest against an unjust but popular war and the immoral but popular institution of slave-owning. He did more than write—he declined to pay his taxes, and was hauled off to gaol in consequence. Who can say how much this refusal of his hastened the end of the war and of slavery ?

Law   **ISBN:** *1-59462-747-9*   **Pages:48**

MSRP $7.45

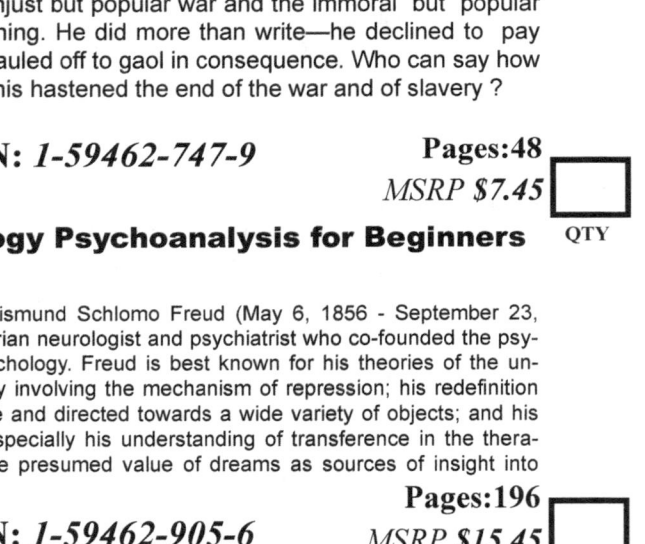

Dream Psychology Psychoanalysis for Beginners
Sigmund Freud

QTY

Sigmund Freud, born Sigismund Schlomo Freud (May 6, 1856 - September 23, 1939), was a Jewish-Austrian neurologist and psychiatrist who co-founded the psychoanalytic school of psychology. Freud is best known for his theories of the unconscious mind, especially involving the mechanism of repression; his redefinition of sexual desire as mobile and directed towards a wide variety of objects; and his therapeutic techniques, especially his understanding of transference in the therapeutic relationship and the presumed value of dreams as sources of insight into unconscious desires.

Pages:196

Psychology   **ISBN:** *1-59462-905-6*   *MSRP $15.45*

The Miracle of Right Thought
Orison Swett Marden

QTY

Believe with all of your heart that you will do what you were made to do. When the mind has once formed the habit of holding cheerful, happy, prosperous pictures, it will not be easy to form the opposite habit. It does not matter how improbable or how far away this realization may see, or how dark the prospects may be, if we visualize them as best we can, as vividly as possible, hold tenaciously to them and vigorously struggle to attain them, they will gradually become actualized, realized in the life. But a desire, a longing without endeavor, a yearning abandoned or held indifferently will vanish without realization.

Pages:360

Self Help   **ISBN:** *1-59462-644-8*   *MSRP $25.45*

The Rosicrucian Cosmo-Conception Mystic Christianity by *Max Heindel*   ISBN: *1-59462-188-8*   **$38.95**
The Rosicrucian Cosmo-conception is not dogmatic, neither does it appeal to any other authority than the reason of the student. It is not controversial, but is: sent forth in the, hope that it may help to clear...   New Age/Religion Pages 646

Abandonment To Divine Providence by *Jean-Pierre de Caussade*   ISBN: *1-59462-228-0*   **$25.95**
"The Rev. Jean Pierre de Caussade was one of the most remarkable spiritual writers of the Society of Jesus in France in the 18th Century. His death took place at Toulouse in 1751. His works have gone through many editions and have been republished...   Inspirational/Religion Pages 400

Mental Chemistry by *Charles Haanel*   ISBN: *1-59462-192-6*   **$23.95**
Mental Chemistry allows the change of material conditions by combining and appropriately utilizing the power of the mind. Much like applied chemistry creates something new and unique out of careful combinations of chemicals the mastery of mental chemistry...   New Age Pages 354

The Letters of Robert Browning and Elizabeth Barret Barrett 1845-1846 vol II   ISBN: *1-59462-193-4*   **$35.95**
by *Robert Browning* and *Elizabeth Barrett*   Biographies Pages 596

Gleanings In Genesis (volume I) by *Arthur W. Pink*   ISBN: *1-59462-130-6*   **$27.45**
Appropriately has Genesis been termed "the seed plot of the Bible" for in it we have, in germ form, almost all of the great doctrines which are afterwards fully developed in the books of Scripture which follow...   Religion/Inspirational Pages 420

The Master Key by *L. W. de Laurence*   ISBN: *1-59462-001-6*   **$30.95**
In no branch of human knowledge has there been a more lively increase of the spirit of research during the past few years than in the study of Psychology, Concentration and Mental Discipline. The requests for authentic lessons in Thought Control, Mental Discipline and...   New Age/Business Pages 422

The Lesser Key Of Solomon Goetia by *L. W. de Laurence*   ISBN: *1-59462-092-X*   **$9.95**
This translation of the first book of the "Lemegton" which is now for the first time made accessible to students of Talismanic Magic was done, after careful collation and edition, from numerous Ancient Manuscripts in Hebrew, Latin, and French...   New Age/Occult Pages 92

Rubaiyat Of Omar Khayyam by *Edward Fitzgerald*   ISBN: *1-59462-332-5*   **$13.95**
Edward Fitzgerald, whom the world has already learned, in spite of his own efforts to remain within the shadow of anonymity, to look upon as one of the rarest poets of the century, was born at Bredfield, in Suffolk, on the 31st of March, 1809. He was the third son of John Purcell...   Music Pages 172

Ancient Law by *Henry Maine*   ISBN: *1-59462-128-4*   **$29.95**
The chief object of the following pages is to indicate some of the earliest ideas of mankind, as they are reflected in Ancient Law, and to point out the relation of those ideas to modern thought.   Religion/History Pages 452

Far-Away Stories by *William J. Locke*   ISBN: *1-59462-129-2*   **$19.45**
"Good wine needs no bush, but a collection of mixed vintages does. And this book is just such a collection. Some of the stories I do not want to remain buried for ever in the museum files of dead magazine-numbers an author's not unpardonable vanity..."   Fiction Pages 272

Life of David Crockett by *David Crockett*   ISBN: *1-59462-250-7*   **$27.45**
"Colonel David Crockett was one of the most remarkable men of the times in which he lived. Born in humble life, but gifted with a strong will, an indomitable courage, and unremitting perseverance...   Biographies/New Age Pages 424

Lip-Reading by *Edward Nitchie*   ISBN: *1-59462-206-X*   **$25.95**
Edward B. Nitchie, founder of the New York School for the Hard of Hearing, now the Nitchie School of Lip-Reading, Inc, wrote "LIP-READING Principles and Practice". The development and perfecting of this meritorious work on lip-reading was an undertaking...   How-to Pages 400

A Handbook of Suggestive Therapeutics, Applied Hypnotism, Psychic Science   ISBN: *1-59462-214-0*   **$24.95**
by *Henry Munro*   Health/New Age/Health/Self-help Pages 376

A Doll's House: and Two Other Plays by *Henrik Ibsen*   ISBN: *1-59462-112-8*   **$19.95**
Henrik Ibsen created this classic when in revolutionary 1848 Rome. Introducing some striking concepts in playwriting for the realist genre, this play has been studied the world over.   Fiction/Classics/Plays 308

The Light of Asia by *sir Edwin Arnold*   ISBN: *1-59462-204-3*   **$13.95**
In this poetic masterpiece, Edwin Arnold describes the life and teachings of Buddha. The man who was to become known as Buddha to the world was born as Prince Gautama of India but he rejected the worldly riches and abandoned the reigns of power when...   Religion/History/Biographies Pages 170

The Complete Works of Guy de Maupassant by *Guy de Maupassant*   ISBN: *1-59462-157-8*   **$16.95**
"For days and days, nights and nights, I had dreamed of that first kiss which was to consecrate our engagement, and I knew not on what spot I should put my lips..."   Fiction/Classics Pages 240

The Art of Cross-Examination by *Francis L. Wellman*   ISBN: *1-59462-309-0*   **$26.95**
Written by a renowned trial lawyer, Wellman imparts his experience and uses case studies to explain how to use psychology to extract desired information through questioning.   How-to/Science/Reference Pages 408

Answered or Unanswered? by *Louisa Vaughan*   ISBN: *1-59462-248-5*   **$10.95**
Miracles of Faith in China   Religion Pages 112

The Edinburgh Lectures on Mental Science (1909) by *Thomas*   ISBN: *1-59462-008-3*   **$11.95**
This book contains the substance of a course of lectures recently given by the writer in the Queen Street Hall, Edinburgh. Its purpose is to indicate the Natural Principles governing the relation between Mental Action and Material Conditions...   New Age/Psychology Pages 148

Ayesha by *H. Rider Haggard*   ISBN: *1-59462-301-5*   **$24.95**
Verily and indeed it is the unexpected that happens! Probably if there was one person upon the earth from whom the Editor of this, and of a certain previous history, did not expect to hear again...   Classics Pages 380

Ayala's Angel by *Anthony Trollope*   ISBN: *1-59462-352-X*   **$29.95**
The two girls were both pretty, but Lucy who was twenty-one who supposed to be simple and comparatively unattractive, whereas Ayala was credited, as her Bombwhat romantic name might show, with poetic charm and a taste for romance. Ayala when her father died was nineteen...   Fiction Pages 484

The American Commonwealth by *James Bryce*   ISBN: *1-59462-286-8*   **$34.45**
An interpretation of American democratic political theory. It examines political mechanics and society from the perspective of Scotsman James Bryce   Politics Pages 572

Stories of the Pilgrims by *Margaret P. Pumphrey*   ISBN: *1-59462-116-0*   **$17.95**
This book explores pilgrims religious oppression in England as well as their escape to Holland and eventual crossing to America on the Mayflower, and their early days in New England...   History Pages 268

www.**bookjungle**.com *email: sales@bookjungle.com fax: 630-214-0564 mail: Book Jungle PO Box 2226 Champaign, IL 61825*

QTY

The Fasting Cure *by Sinclair Upton*　　　　　　　　　　　ISBN: *1-59462-222-1*　**$13.95**
*In the Cosmopolitan Magazine for May, 1910, and in the Contemporary Review (London) for April, 1910, I published an article dealing with my experi-
ences in fasting. I have written a great many magazine articles, but never one which attracted so much attention...*　New Age/Self Help/Health Pages 164

Hebrew Astrology *by Sepharial*　　　　　　　　　　　　ISBN: *1-59462-308-2*　**$13.45**
*In these days of advanced thinking it is a matter of common observation that we have left many of the old landmarks behind and that we are now pressing
forward to greater heights and to a wider horizon than that which represented the mind-content of our progenitors...*　Astrology Pages 144

Thought Vibration or The Law of Attraction in the Thought World　　ISBN: *1-59462-127-6*　**$12.95**

by William Walker Atkinson　　　　　　　　　　　　　　Psychology/Religion Pages 144

Optimism *by Helen Keller*　　　　　　　　　　　　　　ISBN: *1-59462-108-X*　**$15.95**
*Helen Keller was blind, deaf, and mute since 19 months old, yet famously learned how to overcome these handicaps, communicate with the world, and
spread her lectures promoting optimism. An inspiring read for everyone...*　Biographies/Inspirational Pages 84

Sara Crewe *by Frances Burnett*　　　　　　　　　　　ISBN: *1-59462-360-0*　**$9.45**
*In the first place, Miss Minchin lived in London. Her home was a large, dull, tall one, in a large, dull square, where all the houses were alike, and all the
sparrows were alike, and where all the door-knockers made the same heavy sound...*　Childrens/Classic Pages 88

The Autobiography of Benjamin Franklin *by Benjamin Franklin*　　ISBN: *1-59462-135-7*　**$24.95**
*The Autobiography of Benjamin Franklin has probably been more extensively read than any other American historical work, and no other book of its kind
has had such ups and downs of fortune. Franklin lived for many years in England, where he was agent...*　Biographies/History Pages 332

Name	
Email	
Telephone	
Address	
City, State ZIP	

☐ **Credit Card**　　　　　　☐ **Check / Money Order**

Credit Card Number	
Expiration Date	
Signature	

Please Mail to:　Book Jungle
　　　　　　　　PO Box 2226
　　　　　　　　Champaign, IL 61825
or Fax to:　　　630-214-0564

ORDERING INFORMATION

web*: www.bookjungle.com*
email*: sales@bookjungle.com*
fax*: 630-214-0564*
mail*: Book Jungle PO Box 2226 Champaign, IL 61825*
or PayPal *to sales@bookjungle.com*

Please contact us for bulk discounts

DIRECT-ORDER TERMS

**20% Discount if You Order
Two or More Books**
Free Domestic Shipping!
Accepted: Master Card, Visa,
Discover, American Express